About This

Let's talk about Death.
After all, it's the one thing we all have in common. Eventually.
Then let's write stories about it...

Twenty authors have done exactly that, giving you twenty- eight tales on the one subject no-one wants to talk about, but everyone knows they can't avoid.

Whether it's clear guidance on how to handle humans in another world, the story of a man who has no idea he is dead, a true account of saying goodbye to Dad, or making lipsmacking use of a departed friend, this collection explores Death in its many different guises – offering brilliant takes on old mortality: from the spine-tingling, scary and screwy to the strange, touching and poignant.

Often creepy, sometimes funny, always surprising, the stories in this book were drawn from the massive network of talent connected with Portsmouth Writers' Hub, and boasts internationally-published authors as well as talented newcomers to the printed page.

Shudder, weep, laugh... and enjoy; the authors of the Day of the Dead invite you to join their celebration of all things mortal - before it's too late...

Books from Life Is Amazing with a Portsmouth theme

Fiction
The Three Belles Star in "We'll Meet Again"
Turn The Tides Gently (ebook)
The Song of Miss Tolstoy (ebook)
Portsmouth Fairy Tales for Grown-Ups
By Celia's Arbour
(by Walter Besant and James Rice)
Dark City (edited by Karl Bell & Stephen Pryde-Jarman)

Non-Fiction
Conan Doyle and the Mysterious World of Light, 1887-1920
(by Matt Wingett)
Ten Years In A Portsmouth Slum
(by Robert Dolling, edited by Matt Wingett)
The History of Portsmouth
(by Lake Allen, edited by Matt Wingett)
Recollections of John Pounds
(by Henry Hawkes, newspaper extracts collated by Matt Wingett)

DAY OF THE DEAD

by members of

Portsmouth Writers' Hub

edited by

Matt Wingett

Tessa Ditner

William Sutton

Life Is Amazing

A Life Is Amazing Paperback

Day of the Dead

First published 2016 by Life Is Amazing
ISBN: 978-0-9956394-1-6
First Edition

Dedication:

To the amazingly varied voices who make up the creative world of Portsmouth Writers' Hub. To the power of each unique imagination, and to the stories you create. Also, to William Sutton and the Day of the Dead events he runs, where shivers lurk in the shadows, and tingles run up and down your spine.

Acknowledgements

A huge thank you to all the writers who contributed to this collection and to Jon Everitt for his wonderful cover art. Thanks should also go to the team of editors who supported each other through this book, including Tessa Ditner, Will Sutton, Diana Bretherick, Matt Wingett and Jo West. A special mention should go to Andy Brown for his excellent proof-reading skills and to everyone who has been so supportive of this project. Tessa should also get a special mention again for being such an inspiration to Portsmouth Writers' Hub – and to New Writing South for showing interest in our work.

Contents

Introduction

I'm always fascinated by how *where* you're reading adds something to *what* you're reading. I opened 'Day of the Dead' on a long train journey along the South Coast on a dark, cold October night. Everything seemed comfortable enough when I left Brighton, but by the time I hit Rye at page 46, I couldn't have felt more unsettled!

Setting – in the form of Portsmouth – has been integral to the 'Day of the Dead' project and to all the writers involved.

About 3 years ago, writer William Sutton imagined it would be fun to run a Hallowe'en event where Portsmouth writers would get together and perform their stories to the public...

Picture the medieval Square Tower in Old Portsmouth, down by the crashing sea. It is another dark October night. Now imagine these tales being brought to life by a sombre gathering of writers (even though they were actually having a brilliant time!) The Tower was full that night and has been since for annual events celebrating the ghoulish, dark and macabre.

On a lighter note, 'Day of the Dead' is also a celebration of the literary talent and endeavour that is very much ALIVE in Portsmouth today. The project is a great example of the work of The Portsmouth Writers' Hub, which has been such a mobilising force for writers and writing in the city. In these pages you'll find the work of established authors and poets alongside complete beginners, all bringing a fresh perspective to the eternal theme of death.

It has been wonderful to see the Portsmouth Writers Hub evolve in recent years, in association with New Writing South. Portsmouth now really stands out as a place where writers are bringing so much to each other and to the city where they live and write. New Writing South is thrilled to be involved with Portsmouth and is championing this collective and inclusive approach to writing around the region.

Thanks are due to Will Sutton for his energy and inspiration in leading this project, to Tessa Ditner for her tireless dedication to the Portsmouth Writers' Hub, to Matt Wingett for publishing the book, and to all the contributing writers.

Portsmouth really does have a thriving literary scene. In the footsteps of Charles Dickens, H.G. Wells, Rudyard Kipling and Sir Arthur Conan Doyle - all of whom had connections to the city and knew how to pen an unsettling tale! – I imagine there will be many Portsmouth writers today haunting the readers of the future.

Whether you read 'Day of the Dead' in a lively café or a deathly station, at midnight or midday, in Portsmouth or beyond, I hope these tales give you the shivers and maybe even the inspiration to write your own...

Don't have nightmares.

John Prebble
New Writing South
October 2016

DAY OF THE DEAD

Missive hereafter

Maggie Sawkins

Many owners keep their human alone in a bedsit or flat. This leads to a miserable life. Humans have complex social lives and are happiest in company – therefore, humans should ideally live in friendly pairs or groups. However, keeping the wrong pairings together can lead to unwanted offspring and/or fighting. The best combination is a castrated male and a sterilised female. Even two castrated males are likely to fight, as humans are territorial. Sterilising prevents unwanted pregnancies and can reduce fighting.

If you are thinking of getting another human, please speak to your local authority first. They will be able to help ensure you can meet the needs of a pair. Unfamiliar humans need to be introduced to each other gradually and under supervision, preferably in a space that is new to both. Lack of an interesting environment, opportunities to exercise, appropriate company and mental stimulation can lead humans to display abnormal behaviours including hair plucking, head banging, and hoarding.

When handling humans, you should remember they are ground-living creatures who can find being lifted and carried distressing. Owners should approach from the same level rather than from above. When picking up your human ensure that its two legs and bottom are securely supported at all times.

Remember: Humans should never be picked up by the scruff of the neck.

Waste not, want not

S J Butler

We'd have a sit down and a little slug of whisky in our tea to get the day going. Lines the stomach just right. And we always liked to have a bit of a chat before we got down to work.

Right up till a couple of year ago there was just us three at the allotments. Oh there was a flash in the pan back in the seventies – all that Good Life nonsense – men with beards and no muscles, useless for digging. Brought their women too. Ours didn't come near. They didn't last, mind. There one week, gone the next. Left perfectly good crops in the ground, some of them – those that managed to grow any. That made us mad, that did. You couldn't take them, those lettuces and carrots, in case the beardy people came back. And when they didn't, it broke our hearts to see it all go to waste. Not that we were short of lettuces, mind. Even allowing for the damn rabbits, we had plenty.

So what I'm saying is that we'd stuck together, dug together, our whole lives almost. Those two knew me better even than Ada did – I told them things that would have made her blush. Or shout and bang pans. You talk differently to your mates, don't you? If you've shared your best tools, sheltered side by side in the shed against the rain for sixty odd year, you get close.

Of course, we knew none of us was getting any younger. Stands to reason one of us had to go, sooner or later. Well, sooner, to be honest. And they're wrong, those newspapers, when they say people don't talk about death in this country. Maybe those fancy journalist types don't, but we'd all seen death close up, saw it coming too, and we weren't afraid to chew it over. – How we'd prefer to go. What shoes we'd wear in our coffins. Wellies or best? – not an easy one. What we'd want the others to do if we turned into dribbling cabbages. A quick thump with a shovel won that one. Oh yes, we were quite comfortable talking about our deaths. It was a laugh, no doubt about it.

Still, it came as one hell of a shock – excuse my French – when it happened. Run over by a truck on that corner by the Co-op, he was. Bang! – and Bill was gone. One hell of a shock. He was the youngest of us – only 78, he was, and strong too. A bit hard of hearing – probably why he didn't hear that truck – but sound as a bell otherwise. We knew what to do, though. We'd planned it all out over our tea and whisky. So the evening after the funeral, we got to work.

That was a long night, I can tell you. But our promise to Bill kept us going. We had to do right by him. And we'd invited that many people, we couldn't pull out. So we used every bit of Bill's produce and made a feast. We started off digging to lift it out of the ground. Then chopping, cutting, peeling, boiling, roasting... we were fit to drop by morning.

Come first light we loaded it up into barrows, piled high as we dared – meat on the bottom, cooked veg above, and salads on top – and wheeled the whole lot down to the allotments. Three round trips it took. And we had to hurry to get it all set up by lunchtime. Nearly had a disaster on the kerb outside my house, but we reloaded and by twelve midday we were sitting in our chairs drinking tea, and toasting Bill with a slug of whisky. It did look good – we'd done him proud.

The first lot arrived bang on time – it was those young ones from next the post office. You know – they took the plot next to mine a couple of years back. I could see how impressed they were – as well they should have been, given the state of their plot. Decent young people though, always happy to listen and learn, and they tucked straight in.

The rest arrived in short order – almost a hundred in all, every one of them an allotmenteer. After years with the whole place to ourselves, allotments got popular again – every plot was taken. There was even a waiting list. I wasn't too sure I liked it myself – it's all well and good people getting keen about growing, and I'm the first man to say it's the best thing to spend your time doing – but we had no peace. Always asking questions, they were: 'Mr Todd, how deep do you sow your cabbages?' 'Mr T, where have all the flowers gone on my beans?' I don't know – they don't seem to know anything useful these days, the young people. But they were good hearted folk, and they were starting to pick up the ways of allotmenteering. Not just how to sow seeds and the like. The way of doing things proper. You know, make do and mend. Bodge don't buy. Waste not, want not.

I think they were pretty struck by our feast. Didn't have us down as cooks, maybe. You can't beat a good roast, I always say. And this was the best quality meat – well matured, local, reared in the fresh air on good greens. Plenty of it too, luckily, with such a crowd.

We'd baked the ribs in a sticky rich sauce and they went down a treat, all 24 of them. We'd thought about roasting the legs and arms whole, but thought we'd better chop them up into steaks, and mince them for burgers. We made a lovely liver stew – all that whisky had built it up a treat, no doubt about it. And my old mother's recipe for brawn came in handy for the rest. Though it took us all night, we did him proud. Waste not, want not, as Bill always said. And we didn't.

Kissing him goodbye

Glenda Cooper

I am now officially worth four guineas. That's three guineas and twenty bob more than anyone would pay for me before I bobbed head down along the Thames.

It is early morning. The mist is skimming the surface of the river, the watermen are rubbing their eyes as they unloop the ropes that tie the wherries to the bank.

My forehead grazes against wood. The planks leave a red kiss on my skin. My red curls snake out. I begin to drift away from the bank back into the faster flowing water.

But there is a shout and someone snatches at my filthy skirts.

"'S a woman"

The wherry rocks and slices against my arm.

"Comeoncomeoncomeon."

A rough, gruff voice – followed by a pull on my arm, then a grasp of my bodice. With a succession of bumps I land in the stinking bottom of the boat. Sweat, urine, bad beer; gah. They turn me over; my sightless eyes face them.

Immediately there is a high-pitched gabble of benediction, a belch and the unmistakable smell of vomit – a young lad I would guess: seeing his first body.

But the others are tougher. One runs his hands over my body greedily, looking for a concealed pocket, a locket, a handkerchief of coins. His fingers prod the contours of my shape, grasp at my breasts but he finds nothing. He howls as he is pushed aside. My arm is lifted up and held to a bristly cheek.

"Still warm – just. We need to get her to the Duke's Head. Jem, for Christ's sake stop spewing."

There is a sob, another belch and a bout of swearing.

*

Everyone at the Duke's Head, Putney has read the notice that Dr William Hawes has nailed to the lintel.

Society for the Recovery of
Persons Apparently Drowned.
Instructions:

1. Immediately THE OBJECT is removed from the water; blankets or greatcoats are to be wrapped around the body, which is to then to be conveyed with care to the nearest receiving house.

2. IN COLD OR MOIST WEATHER the body is to be laid on a mattress or bed near the fire.

The puckering of my skin continues, despite the two greatcoats. My head lolls back, bouncing against the waterman's upper arm as they scuttle up to the inn in excitement.

I can hear the calls for Dr Hawes. He has primed people like my waterman all along the river, offered them a reward for *all those who will attempt to recover man, woman or child taken for dead from the water, provided they have not been under the water for more than two hours.*

What they care about is this: *There are four guineas on offer if the patient is restored to life.* Close on a year's wages for a housemaid, a good six months for a labourer, or almost enough for a good bay gelding if you're gentry.

So for once, I'm given the treatment due to a fine lady; no more sly kicks, slaps or spitting in my face. No, this time my body is rubbed with salt, a flannel sprinkled with rum is laid to my breast, my wrists are massaged with brandy, a heated brick blisters my foot.

And directing all this is Jack Delinpole, eldest son of the house, wastrel, liar. Jack Delinpole, whom I'd loved from an early age and who'd traded on it; who'd told me he'd look after me but turned pimp.

Now he pushes the waterman aside, and swears.

"Nell?" His voice is faint.

"Is Dr Hawes coming?" he asks, as he brushes back the tendrils of hair that have stuck to my forehead, and bends over me.

I have dreamed a hundred times of this. There is no pain this time, no insults spat in my ear. Instead his fingers are skimming the hairs on my arms, tracing the pulse on my neck, and then his lips press down on mine.

He jumps back and my head bounces back on the mattress.

"Eurgh....shite," he exclaims. "There's half the Thames in there."

He bends over my body once more. Then I realise why; the sound of an educated man, querulous and excited. Jack steps back and Dr Hawes' periwig laps against my forehead. In the Duke's Head they make jokes about him – a madman who talks about pneumatic chemistry in dephlogisticated air, in blowing breath to revive the body when all right-thinking people know that to embrace a corpse is to embrace the noxious fumes that killed them.

Still four guineas is four guineas. For that Jack Delinpole would kiss a flea-pocked dog.

So his kiss now is not for any love of my fine eyes. So I should be glad that his touch now feels no more substantial to me than the skittering of a waterstrider across the river's surface, that the barley taste of his tongue is melting and slipping off my lips.

"She's breathing!" he says. And then adds uncertainly: "Isn't she?"

And they all crowd round now, the learned doctor beating them back "No more than six people! No more than six – pure air is essential."

And even though it is harder to hear, and the world is more blurred and the scents that filled my nose before have vaporised, there is a speck in time when I consider ignoring the inviting call of an endless sleep.

And then I think: what is the best revenge?

And so, Jack, I don't breathe.

Skein and bone

V H Leslie

They parted company at Paris Gare Montparnasse, Laura and Libby waving goodbye to Jess who stood with her coterie of male admirers. Laura was only pretending to wave goodbye to Jess and the boys; it was Paris that she was really bidding farewell. Libby, on the other hand, waved enthusiastically to her friends on the platform, regretting already that she had agreed to leave. As if to confirm her misgivings, Luc kissed Jess on the cheek and the other boys jostled around, eager to impress her now that Libby was gone. They didn't look back. And as the train pulled out of the station, Libby wished for a moment that she didn't have a sister.

Laura sat at her side, a book already open on her lap.

'Happy now?' Libby said.

'You didn't have to come. I'm quite capable of going on my own.'

'Yeah, and Mum would be really happy about that.'

'Your choice.'

Laura always had to have the last word so Libby responded by switching on her iPod and crossing her arms. 'Wake me up when we're there.'

Laura nodded but didn't take her eyes off her guidebook. She was used to her sister's moods and wasn't going to allow it to affect the trip. She hadn't allowed it to affect things so far, though her sister had been particularly obstinate since their arrival in Paris. When Libby teamed up with her best friend Jess, trouble usually followed and Laura was under no illusions that their mother had insisted on Laura's going as a way of restraining them. Laura was bookish and dependable, the sobering presence in their trio. And though Libby was quite free-spirited, as the older sibling she maintained an iota of responsibility with her sister in tow.

But the boys they'd met in Paris had proven a challenge. Jess had been smitten with Luc straight away and Libby enjoyed being surrounded by young men. They'd already extended their time in Paris. Laura didn't mind at first, as it allowed her time to peruse the art galleries at her leisure (while her sister and Jess sat in cafés drinking and smoking their student loans away) but it didn't leave a lot of time to see the rest of France.

When Luc had suggested that they leave the youth hostel to stay in his apartment in the Latin Quarter Laura thought it really was time to go. What she couldn't understand was that her sister had actually considered the offer and that without Laura's voice of reason, Libby would now be shacked up with Jess and a load of Parisian boys.

Perhaps that was why her sister was so pissed at her.

They had never been very alike. People always talk about unbreakable bonds between sisters but Libby and Laura had always just tolerated each other. Libby was beautiful and very aware of it, with naturally golden hair that fell in waves to her shoulders. Laura was happy to admit that she was fairly plain, as if all the beauty in her parent's genetic recipe had been exhausted in the creation of their firstborn, but she prided herself on her intellect. A far greater asset, she reasoned, viewing the attainments of the mind more pressing than the pursuits of the flesh. Laura poured over books while Libby chased boys. Even their mother looked at them quizzically sometimes, as if she couldn't believe they had both come from the same space in her womb.

Jess however wasn't bound by sibling duty so she opted to stay in Paris until the end of the week and then meet the girls in La Rochelle. Laura didn't like Jess. She was a constant reminder of what her sister could become if left to cultivate her vanity and arrogance. But perhaps Libby wasn't beyond saving.

*

'Votre billet, s'il vous plaît.'

Libby woke with a start to a young conductor waiting. The seat beside her was empty.

'Um. Sorry. Excusez-moi.' She looked through her sister's

backpack. Laura was always in charge of the documents and paperwork. It was one of the perks of having her along on the trip, plus she had the best French. She was the reliable one.

The conductor looked at his watch.

Laura returned and handed the conductor the tickets from her pocket. He punched them and gave them back.

'Where have you been?' Libby asked.

'To get some food. Want some?' She dropped a cellophane wrapped baguette into her lap.

'Why didn't you wake me?'

'You said not to wake you until we got there.'

'You're so pedantic. Don't sneak off, ok?'

'I've been on my own in Paris for nearly three weeks, I think I can manage.'

'Whatever.' Libby stretched. 'You were in art galleries. You're not as worldly wise as me.'

'Clearly.'

'Hey!' She raised an eyebrow at her sister, an expression she used occasionally to remind Laura that she was the eldest and therefore in charge. If she knew how it furrowed her forehead she probably wouldn't do it. She opened the baguette and took a bite. Then she pulled a magazine out of her bag and flicked through the pages. She folded back the corners, a habit she had for when she saw an outfit she liked. Not that she could afford the price tag of many of the garments gracing the glossy pages. Or, for that matter, the clothes that adorned the shop windows in all those little Parisian boutiques that had mercilessly lured her. She'd decided that when she got home she was going to uncover her mother's sewing machine in the loft, perhaps take some lessons at the local college. After all, imitation is the highest form of flattery.

'What are you reading?' Laura asked.

'Vogue.'

'It's in French.'

'So? The language of fashion is universal.'

Laura rolled her eyes but peered at the double-page spread anyway. It featured a group of anorexic models in animal print. 'What's she wearing?'

'Dior.'

'Looks more like a zebra.'

'It's the fashion.'

'Well she looks more like a fashion victim,' Laura observed, 'but not as much as the zebra.' She chuckled at her own joke, only stopping when she saw her sister's eyebrow rise again. She returned to her guidebook instead. 'I didn't realise but we're passing through a small village that has a really awesome château.'

'Uh huh.' Libby didn't look up from her magazine.

'It says, The house is a resplendent example of Renaissance architecture, notable for its association with the Court of Louis XV and for playing host to some of the most lavish balls of the eighteenth century.'

Libby turned the pages of her magazine but Laura could tell the lavish balls had her attention.

'Why don't we get off there, take a look around and pick up the train later?'

Libby shifted in her seat. 'It's getting late. If it's a small place there might not be a later train.'

'We could catch one tomorrow. We could always stay in a hotel. There's bound to be one if the château is mentioned in here.' She held up the guidebook to support her point.

Libby closed her magazine with a sigh. 'It could be deserted.'

'Aren't you always saying I should be more spontaneous?' Laura insisted. 'You know, like you?'

Libby shook her head.

'It also has.' Laura traced the text with her finger, skim reading, 'a library, an ornamental garden, an aviary and er... an unsurpassed collection of period costume.'

'Ok, ok. Just a few hours. Then we'll carry on to La Rochelle.'

'Fine.'

When the train pulled into the next station they were the only two to get off.

*

'There has to be a mistake,' Laura said as she thumped the pages of her guidebook once more.

'Brilliant,' Libby said, taking the last warm swig of mineral water.

She had made a seat for herself from their luggage and was watching her sister with increasing irritation. They were camped in front of large wrought iron gates. A sign reading 'Fermé' in large red lettering hung from the bars. Laura peered through to the château beyond.

The road to the château had been difficult; there were few signposts and the château itself was hardly mentioned. They'd followed a sketchy map in the guidebook but the book was old and many of the street names were omitted. Added to this, the village seemed pretty deserted. They passed derelict buildings, run down farmland and neglected vineyards, seeing only the occasional inhabitant whose directions to the château had been likewise vague. On top of this, the day had been unexpectedly humid. Even now, in the gathering dusk, the heat remained like a heady, suffocating weight. Their clothes clung to them and the dust from the road had seemed somehow to stick to their skin, getting between their toes and on their lips. They licked it away but could taste the red earth.

It became clear that there was no hotel or bed and breakfast and it was looking increasingly likely that they would be spending the night sleeping on a bench in the railway station.

'What do we do now?' Laura asked.

'I don't know. You're the one with all the answers.'

'I thought it would be open. I thought there would be a later train or at least somewhere to stay.' She sat on the ground beside her sister. She thought back to the train station. To the tourist information and accommodation guides in the revolving bookstand next to the ticket office. That she hadn't picked up.

'Usually I plan things a bit more.'

'Spontaneous doesn't suit everyone,' Libby replied. 'Ok, here's what we'll do, we'll head back to the station and on the way we'll knock on a few doors and see if anyone knows of a hotel or something.'

'I feel funny about knocking on people's doors.'

'You're the one who made us get off the train.'

'Ok. Ok.'

'It's starting to rain,' Libby announced as she began to gather her things.

'No it's not,' Laura replied. But as she reached out her arm for her backpack she felt it. It was replenishing at first but within the space of a few minutes it fell in floods, intent on washing away the humidity.

'Let's go,' Libby called.

Laura nodded but gripped the railings. 'It's just so annoying. We came all this way.' She rattled the bars in frustration and was surprised when the latch gave way. The gate opened ever so slightly, though still secured by the chain. It was wide enough for a person to squeeze through.

Libby looked at Laura.

'No way,' Laura began, 'it says it's closed.'

'I'm only going to have a quick look.'

And with that she slid between the gap.

*

Even in the diminishing light, and even with the rain, it was clear to see that the garden was overgrown and neglected. Laura could make out a variety of topiary shapes lining the path, their forms vaguely familiar. They looked like birds. Some seemed to lean over, their beaks in the ground as if rummaging for food. Others seemed to stand upright, pushing out their chests, perched high on their circular platforms. And finally, at the front of the house, two peacocks sat either side of the entrance. They guarded it like beautiful gargoyles, their fan of feathers spread out like a hand of playing cards, their eyes ever watchful.

The château was a grand, impressive building. It was built in the Renaissance style, composed of pilasters and large windows and topped with cylindrical turrets. In the dusk, the slate roof, illuminated by the moon, appeared almost blue. The château looked like a smaller version of the Château de Chenonceau they had visited in the Loire Valley when they first arrived; back when Laura still had some influence over the places they visited as a group. Laura had wanted to see it because it was created by women and designed for the sole purpose of producing aesthetic pleasure. A castle where female aristocrats could play architect, where beauty as opposed to war had governed its construction. Even Libby, not one for heritage sites, had appreciated its grandeur. And here they stood, soaking wet, at the entrance of a building that rivalled it.

Libby took the large brass knocker in her hand.

'What are you doing?'

Libby knocked in response. There was no answer. The rain continued. Libby went to the windows and peered through.

'What can you see?'

'Not much. It's dark.'

'Is anyone there?'

'I don't think so.'

Libby returned and knocked again. She waited a while longer then tried the doorknob. It turned in her hand.

'Wait,' Laura cautioned. 'Wait! We can't go in.'

'Why not? I thought you wanted to see this place?'

'I do, but-'

'C'mon, just for a moment, until the rain stops.' She pushed the door open and stepped inside.

Laura stood a moment longer on the dark veranda then hurried in after her sister.

Libby felt the walls, looking for a light switch. 'Guess there's no electricity then.

'It's probably abandoned.'

'We don't know that.'

Laura followed Libby. The diminishing light shone through the large windows, illuminating the passages. They rounded a corner and found themselves in a large drawing room. It was decorated with high panelled walls, ornate cornicing spiralling out onto the ceiling toward a huge chandelier that refracted the light in glittering pools.

'It's like a castle,' Libby exclaimed. She turned on her heel and darted back into the corridors, swept away on her own tour. She was like a magpie uncovering a nest of shiny treasures. Laura followed steadily behind.

'Wait, hold on, you're going too fast.'

The corridors snaked further into the building, away from the light of the windows. Libby followed the sound of her sister's footsteps. She heard her climb a staircase.

'Wait.'

When she reached the dark landing Laura didn't know which way to go. The house was quiet.

'Libby? Where are you?'

She walked slowly now, a sense of isolation making her cautious. She looked into each room that she passed, hoping she wouldn't find the owner sitting in the darkness. She felt a tightness in her chest, a fluttering anxiety, aware that this was an act of trespass. She needed to get her sister and get out.

She found Libby standing in a room full of people. Laura was so shocked to find the place inhabited that she nearly cried out. But as her eyes became accustomed to the dark she saw that they weren't people but mannequins, dressmaker's dummies donned in the most elaborate costumes.

'Isn't this place amazing?' said Libby.

Laura, intending to reprimand her sister, found instead that she was drawn into the strange room. The mannequins converged around Libby, as if they were gossiping at a grand soiree. Each wore a dress more extravagant than the next. They wore gowns with full skirts scaffolded by panniers and copious petticoats that pushed the fabric out in a billowing mass. They had low, scooped necklines and fitted bodices that emphasized the hourglass figures that had once been so fashionable. They were different by degrees; some had pleated underskirts revealed by decorative loops, whilst others exhibited sleeves that, at the elbows, swelled into layers of frills. One even flaunted a sacque, a loose fold that fell from the shoulder of the garment to the hem, resembling a cape. Each was made of the finest materials. Brocade and silk, voile and velvet, ribbons and lace, tassels and pearls and feathers, all in an array of muted pastels and silvers that glittered in the fading light.

'They must be so old,' Laura said, reaching out to touch the fabric. She expected it to be paper-thin but all the gowns shone with fresh lustre, as if they had just been made.

'It's like the dressing room of Marie Antoinette,' Libby exclaimed. 'Look on the dressing table, you can see the powdered wigs. And there's a selection of hats in the boxes over there.'

'I don't think we should be snooping around.'

'How can we not? This place is amazing. Look in the wardrobe.'

Laura didn't want to, but she opened the door. A crinoline petticoat hung inside like an enormous birdcage. Laura touched one of the hoops; it was strong, reinforced with whalebone, the kind used in the nineteenth century before steel hoops were favoured. But to Laura it reminded her of a medieval torture device she'd seen in a museum in Carcassonne, a gibbet used to detain prisoners as they perished slowly from starvation. The skirt hanging on its railing looked just as torturous.

'This one's my favourite,' Libby declared as Laura closed the wardrobe door. She moved aside to reveal another mannequin. Until now it had been concealed behind her.

Even in the dim light, you could see it wore a gown of red. The skirt, not quite as full as the others, was topped with a corset in burgundy brocade, the edges of which were scalloped into sharp points. It was fastened at the back with a bright red ribbon that tied into a bow at the lower back. It was a fairly simple design compared to the other gowns but there was something devastatingly beautiful about it. Then Laura noticed the waist.

Libby had noticed it too and was caressing the bodice enviously. She liked the way it drew the body in, the way it coerced the shape into such a beautiful silhouette. An impossible waistline.

'Do you know, Scarlett O'Hara's waist was seventeen inches,' Libby said clutching her hands around the mannequin's waistline.

'Scarlett O'Hara was fictional.'

'Still, it was typical of the age.'

'No wonder everyone died so young. Probably of collapsed ribs and compressed internal organs.'

'I think it's beautiful.'

'It's unrealistic and we shouldn't be here.'

'I wonder what it would look like on?'

'No way. What if someone finds us? How would we explain what we're doing?'

'There's no one here,' Libby said, untying the ribbon. She turned to a gilt mirror above a fireplace and stood behind the mannequin, imagining what the corset would look like on. 'Don't you think it would suit me?'

Laura looked in the mirror and met the eyes of her sister's reflection. The red gown seemed to draw out her colour, as if her blood was draining into the gown. Her pallor, now white, made her features strangely cruel.

A blurring at the corner of Laura's eye distracted her from the curious image of her sister. She could make out a shadow in the corner of the room by the door. She looked deeper into the mirror. Had there been a mannequin there? She turned slowly.

A woman stood in the doorway, her face illuminated by the light of a candelabra she held in her hand. Laura jumped and Libby shrieked, releasing the mannequin and the red gown.

'Um, excusez-moi,' Laura stuttered. She drew her phrase book from her pocket and rifled through the pages to disguise her reddening cheeks. Eventually she explained in convoluted French that they were lost.

The woman looked at them both for a moment, as if considering the words. Laura wondered if she'd made a mistake with the pronunciation and after a few more moments, considered that maybe she hadn't uttered a sentence at all. That maybe fear had taken her voice.

Finally the woman moved. She walked towards the red gown, picked up a large sheet that lay discarded on the floor and threw it over the dress. Then she held out an arm and directed them to follow her. They retraced their steps back through the house, the dark corridors brightened now from the light of the candelabra, revealing dozens of portraits on the walls. Staunch-faced relics from a bygone time, left to reside over the labyrinthine passages of the house, watched their departure, for Laura fully expected to be shown the front door. She wouldn't have been surprised if the woman had called the police and she wondered how she would explain the whole episode.

Instead they were directed to a library.

It was a large room and each of the four walls, from the floor to the ceiling was filled with books. Even the inside of the door was papered with their image, like a secret doorway, so that when closed you would be literally immersed. In the centre of the room were four large armchairs arranged around a circular table on which more books were piled, small towers that clearly couldn't fit anywhere else.

The lady instructed them to sit and lit the sconces on the wall and a grand chandelier overhead with a taper. She then busied herself lighting a fire in the stone hearth. All the light emerging allowed Laura and Libby to take in her appearance. She wore a long black dress with a high neck. It looked like the kind of attire a maid or a housekeeper would wear in the nineteenth century. Even her face seemed to bear a strange sense of age, though her body belied it. In fact, there was something curious about her face, not unattractiveness exactly but a kind of emptiness. Perhaps it was merely the mask of servitude, but it was undoubtedly not a face you wanted to look at for very long. With the room now providing an inviting glow the woman withdrew, leaving the girls alone among the leather-bound relics.

'What the hell is going on?' Libby asked in a whisper.

'I'm not sure.'

'Maybe we should go.'

'We can't go now. We've trespassed. There will be consequences.'

'Even more reason to go.'

The woman returned with a silver tray and two small crystal glasses filled with an amber liquid. She offered them.

'Merci,' the girls said in unison.

Laura winced at the taste but it warmed her as much as the fire.

'Asseyez-vous près du feu et je prépare le repas et une chambre pour la nuit,' the housekeeper said softly. Again, Laura had the same strange reluctance to make eye contact. The housekeeper began to leave but paused by the door and turned. 'Excusez la vieille maison, il a beaucoup de souvenirs.' Then she bowed and exited.

'What did she say?' Libby asked once the door was closed, 'I heard something about beds.'

'I think she said that she will prepare us a meal and a room for the night.' They exchanged glances. 'We are to wait here by the fire. Then she said to excuse the house and its memories. I think. Her accent was very strong.'

Libby smiled broadly. 'We've hit the jackpot here.'

Laura frowned. 'It's very hospitable, considering she found us snooping around her house.'

'Perhaps it isn't her house. Did you see the way she was dressed? She looks more like a servant.' Libby leaned forward in her chair. 'Maybe she's being so nice to us because she doesn't want to get into trouble with her master.'

'And why would she get into trouble?'

'Negligence. She left the door open. And the gate wasn't much of an obstacle. Surely it's her job to keep this place secure? It's asking for trouble.'

'And we're the trouble.'

Libby smiled. 'You bet.'

Laura stood and perused the shelves, running her finger along the spines. There were the classic authors one would expect of a library of this kind - Proust and Flaubert, Zola - but there was also an array of non-fiction and political treatises. There was a wealth of knowledge at her fingertips but Laura felt strangely uneasy at the discovery.

Laura reached for a leather-bound copy of Proust's Le Temp Retrouvé and in doing so glimpsed the garden outside. She put the book down and walked to the window. The rain had stopped as if it had merely conspired to get them to inside. A thought that unsettled Laura more than it should have. She could see now how overgrown and neglected the garden was, a sad testament to the spirit of the house. All except for the topiary birds, whose shapes were concrete and precise, the only order amid the confusion. Peering closer, Laura saw that many of the birds were surrounded by willow cloches, constructions designed to shape and curtail their growth. They looked appropriately enough like large birdcages, fashioned to prevent their beautiful captives from taking flight.

'Laura? Why do you think she covered up the red gown?'

Laura could have reasoned that perhaps it was the most expensive, or the oldest, but as with everything about this place Laura was not sure.

*

Dinner was a lavish affair. The housekeeper spoke very little. She instructed the girls to eat, then marched back and forth to the kitchen bringing out a variety of courses on silver platters. Her movements were controlled and considered, graceful despite carrying dishes and plates, a feat perhaps even more noteworthy because of her small frame. She was slight in build and had a wasp-like waist, drawn in by the corset she was undoubtedly wearing underneath her black dress.

The table was laid as if the house were expecting important dignitaries. Silver candelabras ran the length of the table, interspersed by arrangements of wild flowers. Even the crockery was decorated with delicate illustrations of birds of paradise that seemed to flutter eagerly in anticipation of a meal to come. There was more cutlery than they knew what to do with but as soon as the housekeeper placed each meal down, she withdrew, closing the door softly behind her, and so the girls dispensed with manners to grapple with the feast before them.

'Isn't she going to join us?' Laura asked with her mouth full.

'She's clearly a maid. That's what she does. She waits on people. Maybe she thinks we're royalty.'

'It's a bit archaic, don't you think?' But Laura saw that her sister was having no problem at all stomaching their sudden elevation of status.

They feasted on the finest food; *cèpes à la Bordelaise* – mushrooms sautéed with garlic and parsley – before a generous serving of *moules marinières*, which arrived steaming in white wine with shallots. This was followed by *blanquette de veau*– a rich and creamy veal stew – and was concluded with clafoutis. For each course, the housekeeper served a different wine. The meal became a heady, fragrant experience, a gastronomic banquet of tastes and flavours. Libby's lips were stained with merlot.

'What if it's been poisoned,' Laura asked holding up the crystal goblet. They looked at each other a moment before bursting into laughter, the wine making them light-headed and high-spirited.

'I wouldn't care, it tastes too delicious.'

Laura pushed a cherry around her plate with a fork. 'I don't think I can eat another bite.'

'Give it here,' Libby said, 'it's too good to waste.'

They leaned back, nursing their engorged stomachs and licking their lips to recapture the memory of the meal.

'How did they do it?' Laura asked.

'What?'

'Wear corsets like that. Every day.' She undid the top button of her jeans.

'Discipline, I suppose.'

'You wouldn't be able to eat meals like this,' Laura continued, pointing at the empty plates and bowls and glasses strewn before them.

'Unless you were laced in really tight.'

Laura put her hand to her mouth. 'Don't, I'll be sick.'

The housekeeper returned with a tray of strong smelling coffee and a cake stand full of small pastries and chocolates before leaving with yet more empty plates.

'She must have a master,' Laura said when she had gone. 'Where do you suppose they are?'

'Probably away. In Paris, maybe,' said Libby. Laura sensed no resentment, though normally she'd have expected some. 'What does it matter? We're the only ones that count right now.'

*

The housekeeper led the girls back along dark corridors to a bedroom. The rain had renewed its efforts, as if it too had only paused for some supper, and it hammered now against the side of the château, creeping in through the cracks and crevices around the windows and doors, echoing wildly in the belly of the old house.

The bedroom the housekeeper had prepared was an opulent refuge from the storm. The walls were covered with large tapestries that portrayed the Garden of Eden. The weave, in lustrous colours, depicted nature's abundance; fruit in all its wondrous variety hung temptingly from the canvas, ready to be picked. In one, a curvaceous Eve offered the apple enticingly to the viewer. The snake had entwined itself around her, its serpentine body clinging to her waist, emphasising the curve of her hips, and it draped off one shoulder, like an elegantly hung garment, tantalisingly concealing her full nakedness. Below the tapestry, a fire already raged in the stone hearth and a large four-poster bed stood in the centre of the room, adorned with hanging panels of fabric that closed around the bed like a curtain.

'This is awesome,' Libby whispered to Laura.

The housekeeper pointed to an urn and a bowl on the dresser, bowed, and withdrew. Libby dived on the bed.

'I've always wanted to sleep in one of these,' Libby said, 'though I'd never imagined sharing with you.'

Laura wasn't as enthusiastic. She tried to accept the evening as good old-fashioned hospitality but everything had been so extravagant, so superfluous. After what Libby had said about the housekeeper's negligence she had watched her closely. Laura wasn't as concerned about why the house was unlocked as to why it was closed in the first place. It seemed to lack all the features so typical of a tourist hotspot. From what Laura had seen she was beginning to think this place hadn't seen visitors for many years.

The girls dressed for bed and snuggled beneath the covers. The rain against the windowpane only served to make them feel more content in the warm bed.

'Well, this is better than sleeping on a bench at the station,' Libby said merrily. She sat up and began untying a ribbon attached to one of the bedposts.

'Don't pull the curtain down,' Laura said, 'I don't want to feel trapped in here.'

'Don't be silly.'

'Please, I don't like the idea of not seeing a way out.'

Libby shrugged and lay back down.

'It's been a good day,' Libby announced, facing her sister. The coffee had sobered them a degree but Laura wondered if the wine was still exerting its influence on her sister's mood.

'We haven't had a meal like that, just us I mean, for ages.'

Laura nodded.

'I had fun.'

'Me too.'

'And we haven't shared a bed since we were little,' she continued. 'Do you remember?'

Laura nodded, remembering her sister traipsing out of bed in the early hours to sneak into her parents' bed; taking any opportunity to monopolise their parents' love without Laura around. But Laura was woken by the absence of her sister more effectively than any alarm clock. She'd follow her sister into their parents' bed and through the course of the night their fidgeting would force their parents out and up early, leaving the two girls alone in the bed, lingering in the warmth of their parents' bodies.

'I wonder what Jess is up to,' Libby said, breaking her reverie.

'Why do you like her so much?'

Libby thought for a moment. 'She's fun to be around. I know you don't like her, but she's ok.'

'I wish it could be just us sometimes.'

'I know.'

Laura recalled all her lonely meanderings around Paris. The times she had spent with her sister were while she waited outside changing rooms, separated by a curtain as Libby tried on countless outfits. Libby's relationship with her reflection was perhaps more significant than any sisterly bond. 'We've grown so different.'

'C'est la vie,' Libby smiled. 'We're still sisters. We'll always be sisters.'

They looked at each other for a while longer, their faces glowing from the warmth of the fire. The bed was incredibly comfortable and the rain outside a strange lullaby. Laura felt her eyes closing.

'Wouldn't it be great to go back to the dressing room before we leave,' Libby whispered.

Laura stirred. She thought of her lonely tours of the Louvre and the Musée d'Orsay. She'd described the beauty to her sister at dinner but they had been just words to Libby. She couldn't imagine it, and even if she had, she wouldn't have appreciated the aesthetic merit of a group of old paintings anyway.

But how her face had lit up in the dressing room. In the moonlight everything had shimmered like a Moreau painting, misty and iridescent, twinkling as if glimpsed underwater or in a dream. To her sister it was a siren song.

'Promise me you won't go back to that room?' Laura said.

'Why not?'

Laura thought that the contents of that room should be torched. That all those things perpetuated an image of women that was artificial and unrealistic. Those fashions were designed by men to reflect the moral rigidity of the age, to keep women laced in, confined and shackled. The corset signified restraint and conformity, going out of fashion when women's rights were à la mode. Not that things were much different today, in an age of tanning salons and plastic surgery. Society's concept of beauty had always been governed by impossible ideals, usually at the expense of the female body. But she couldn't tell Libby any of that. Her sister hated it when she voiced her feminist leanings. Besides, she was too sleepy and didn't want to spoil the evening's magic.

'Just promise,' was all she said.

'Ok,' Libby conceded. 'Goodnight'

'Goodnight.'

*

Laura found herself in the library. She was sitting in one of the enormous armchairs and the fire smouldered in the grate. In her lap was a copy of Rousseau's Du contrat social. She flicked through the pages, marvelling that the house existed long before such enlightened thinking, when social roles were so clearly delineated.

She put the book down and looked around the room. From her seat, the shelves loomed above her; a vastness of knowledge that was far from liberating. It was intimidating in fact. She stood up and made her way to the door.

Except there was no door. She scanned the room. The door, she remembered, had been papered over with the image of books. She made her way to the corners of the room and felt along the walls, searching for the mystery door. But her hands only touched leather spines. She began to pull them out in frustration. Their paper insides fluttered as they fell to the ground. She ran her hands along the entire length of wall, unable to accept that the door had disappeared. She tried to suppress the alarm mounting inside her. There had to be a way out.

She began pulling greater quantities of books from the shelves, casting them into a growing pile in the centre of the room, an enormous unlit bonfire. She ignored the titles as they flew from shelves, titles that would have ignited her interest at any other time, and she ignored how the books tossed and turned on the ground, flapping and flailing like dying animals. That was when she realised she was dreaming.

With the room stripped of its beauty, all that remained was the skeletal structure of the bookcases, resembling the bars of the crinoline petticoat she'd glimpsed in the dressing room. She ran her hand along the smooth surface and realised they weren't constructed from wood. The shelves were stone, or something else, pale and hard and calcified.

Beyond the bookcases, Laura could make out a door. She stepped between the bars of the bookcase frames and opened it.

She was in the dining room. The table was laid as it had been earlier that day. The cutlery and crockery gleamed and the crystal goblets sparkled. In the centre of the table stood a number of enormous cake-stands, topped with an array of dainty iced cakes and plates of cheeses and fruits crammed every available space. It was a tempting feast. But as she approached she discerned small darting movements. Something rested on her hand and she looked in bewilderment at a tiny bird.

As suddenly as it appeared, it flew from the perch she provided and rejoined the others dancing over the table. There were a dozen or so, darting over the porcelain crockery. Others were nestled on the display of fruit, an edible nest, nimbly feeding as if they were in a garden, leaving small telltale trails of juice and cream and sugar on the white tablecloth. Some darted between the cakes and others perched on the edges of exquisite teacups, dipping their beaks into the tea.

Each of the birds was more beautiful than the next. A parade of plumage. For some their feathers formed skirt-like layers, while others had wings tipped with extraordinary colours, or the most beautiful patterns emblazoned on their chests.

Laura wanted to touch one again.

A shadow moved across the table and the startled birds flew in fright. But they stopped short before they could get far. Their wings beat frantically but they seemed unable to get beyond the orbit of the table.

Laura recoiled as she saw what had frightened them. Between the cake-stand and a teapot, a snake, fat and silver, crept along the table's expanse, knocking against the crockery, causing cakes and pastries to fall from their podiums.

The birds continued to beat their wings but they couldn't fly away. A tangle of red threads covered the feast as fine as cobwebs. She followed a single skein and saw that it was tethered to the foot of a bird. In fact, all the birds were bound by red thread.

The snake coiled around the cake-stand, climbing elegantly despite its heavy body, hauling itself higher and higher. With its jaw distended it made a series of jerking movements in its throat, as if calling to the birds so desperate to flee. A green bird suddenly crashed to the table. It flapped its wings meekly but seemed wounded from the force of its landing. Laura followed the thread and saw it ended, they all ended, in the mouth of the snake, like small arteries. The bird continued to fight and flutter but its attempts became more sporadic and then the snake was suddenly upon it. In one swift movement it swallowed the bird whole.

Laura turned away from the scene in shock and when she turned back the shape of the bird bulged within the reptile's scaly skin, coursing its way down into the body of the beast.

Laura watched with horror as the snake returned to its platform. It opened its jaws, not yet satisfied and the other birds flapped their frenzy.

*

Laura woke up flailing in the bed-sheets. The drapery must have fallen in the night, as she couldn't see beyond the fabric of the bed. She pulled it aside and saw the space beside her empty.

'Libby?'

She looked out into the dark room. Shadows had gathered in the corners, creeping out from behind the tapestries, but otherwise it appeared empty. She knew where her sister would be. Like the birds in her dream, she felt an invisible thread connecting them.

She walked softly but swiftly along the corridors, but the château was vast and she was beginning to think the housekeeper had taken them up a different staircase after dinner. She came to a central stairwell and followed the balustrade, reasoning that if the house were symmetrical this would lead her to all the rooms. Her progress was surveyed by the portraits of the dead, and she wondered how many of them had met their end violently, kneeling at the guillotine or in some other horrible fashion.

She heard a rustle up ahead and quickened her pace. They had trespassed and tested the hospitality of the housekeeper enough already, Laura wanted to retrieve her sister and leave.

In the dressing room, Laura couldn't see her sister at first. She had the same strange impression she was witnessing an extravagant party, the mannequins arranged as if conspiring in the midst of a grand ball. Then Libby stepped out of the crowd, resplendent in the red gown.

'How do I look?'

She looked stunning. The corset drew her body in, her silhouette willowy and delicate. As before, the red of the gown seemed to draw her colour, her skin the sickly, anaemic pallor that was once so fashionable.

Laura couldn't reply but Libby didn't really need an answer. She addressed her reflection and danced in front of the glass as if it were an imaginary dance partner. She twirled, enjoying the feeling of the taffeta as it moved.

'We need to go,' Laura said.

'Ok, ok.' But she continued twirling.

'I'm leaving.'

Libby sighed. It was no fun playing dress up with her sister here. 'Untie me then.'

Laura stood behind her sister and faced the mirror. Beside Libby she appeared so plain. Yet in the glow of the red dress, she noticed that there was a similarity; the arch of her eyebrows, her high cheekbones, her full lips. She was a poor imitation but not without a beauty of her own.

She fumbled with the laces but they were knotted tight.

'How did you do this?'

Libby shrugged. 'I just slipped it on and it settled into place. I only tied it loosely.'

Laura persevered but the laces were taut.

'I don't know what you've done but I can't undo it.'

'Don't pull.'

'I didn't.'

'Stop tugging.'

Laura stepped away. 'I'm not. I didn't touch you.'

Libby shoved her. 'Sure, then why - Ow!' This time she doubled with pain as the laces around her waist tightened. Laura watched as Libby's diaphragm contracted with the force of the material, heard her breath escape in a rush.

'Get it off me!' she gasped.

Laura groped at the laces but they were steadfast. She watched as the ribbon, pulled by invisible hands, tightened further. She tried to stop it but the force was too strong.

'It's tightening on its own!'

Libby clutched her chest, her breath coming in short gasps now. She scratched at the material, trying to rip the corset from her skin. Laura pulled the bodice roughly but it was stiff and unrelenting.

Libby tried to speak but there wasn't enough air in her lungs for words. Her waist contracted again, impossibly sylphlike. She began coughing, only slight sounds, and even in the dim light Laura could see the blood.

Laura looked around the room. Mirror. Dressing table. Wardrobe. She needed something with which to cleave the gown off Libby.

'I'll be right back.'

She made a run for the door but tripped on the hem of a gown and went sprawling. She scrambled on the floor, crawling through layers of fallen silk and taffeta, brushing aside the excessive petticoats of a hundred dressmaker's dummies, layer after layer until she found herself confronted by the bars of a crinoline petticoat. She made to pull it aside-

But couldn't lift it. She tried to turn, to crawl out the other side, but she was enclosed within it, as if it had been lowered over her. She shook the bars of her cage. They didn't feel like the whalebone struts she had touched in the wardrobe. These were not covered in fabric and they were thicker, much thicker, the calcified yellow of bone many centuries old.

Libby's coughing, feeble as it was, suddenly ceased and she collapsed to the floor. She could hear the pop and crunch of her ribs breaking. Laura could see her panting, tiny breaths that gave her nothing. Her eyes were wide. Her chest was stained with blood and it ran down onto the gown. Her waist, impossibly small now, continued to shrink before Laura's eyes.

Laura heard footsteps on the threshold and turned to face the door. The housekeeper stood in the doorway, dressed in a high-necked dressing gown, a candle illuminating her face as she took in the scene before her.

Laura grasped the bars of her tiny prison. 'Help us!'

The housekeeper entered the room slowly, closing the door behind her. She walked toward the dressing table and sat down. Laura watched her movements, reflected in the vanity mirror.

'What are you doing?' Laura called. 'Help us!'

But the housekeeper didn't respond. Instead she began applying white powder to her face, matching her pallor to become the same unnatural shade as Libby's.

'Hey!' Laura called again. 'You have to help us!'

The housekeeper still didn't respond. She removed one of the powdered wigs from its stand and put it on. She was no longer the housekeeper who had welcomed them. She undid her dressing gown and let it slip from her shoulders.

Laura gasped.

Her neck had been slashed open. The flesh parted in a wide gash, a laceration that had long since ceased to bleed but offered instead red threads that unravelled to the floor, each one a degenerate bloodline.

The housekeeper's reflection stared at Laura, her eyebrow raised in displeasure. There was a moment of eye contact, then the housekeeper merely turned away to resume her routine. As if she was dressing for an important occasion.

The housekeeper examined her features in the mirror and ran a finger along the fleshy crevice of her throat, playing the threads like a silent instrument. Her other hand reached into one of the drawers, and withdrew a feather boa of vibrant, exotic feathers. She cast it around her neck and her transformation was complete.

Laura looked around the room in desperation. But the room was changed. Dusty, ruined, the clothes on the mannequins were merely the tattered remains of gowns from a bygone era, cast over the models like shrouds. The paper-thin fabric was frayed at the edges, moth-eaten and yellowing. It was all a masquerade. All but the red gown.

It clung to her sister in her last moments, contracting still.

Laura screamed. She shook the bars of her cage in desperation, stopping only when she felt a sharp tug and a fleeting sensation of pain. She looked down and saw, around her ankle, a single skein of red thread.

(First Published in Black Static # 31, Nov 2012)

The empty stair

Ruth Nelson

"Door. Door. See?" said my toddler, tugging me over. I submitted. With the boy in my arms, I opened our front door and gazed down the empty stairway to the closed door of the building. The wintry evening darkened the stained glass windows set into the heavy wooden frame.

"There. See? There." He pointed confidently to about halfway down the stairs. Then he gazed solemnly, chubby finger out, still and attentive.

The finger began to tentatively waggle. Then the other fingers unfurled and waggled too. They warmed up, waggling with more enthusiasm until his whole hand waved and he smiled, pink mouth full of small white milk teeth. The light over the stairs and the lobby was dim but clear. I, too, gazed solemnly, from him to the empty staircase and back again. His eyes were still held about halfway down the stairs, his mouth still wide in a smile, wisps of blond curl standing out from his head.

"That's enough," I said, and drew us inside, closing the door gently but firmly. We returned to the rhythmic preparation for his bath and bed. The warm glow of lamps held us snug and the sounds from the radio anchored us. A little pair of socks akimbo on the nursery floor led to a little pair of dark blue corduroy trousers discarded by gleefully kicking legs.

"Door. See. Come," he insisted a second time, bare bottomed and firm. We opened the door and again, perched on my hip, he gazed down the empty staircase, one arm stretched out and pointing. "There. See. Lady. There." To my eyes, the stairs held nought but dust and the scuffed patterning of marble risers laid down in the long-vanished years of the 1930s. At length, I drew us back behind our door, feeling the seeping chill of a damp winter. The rush of hot water and the rise of steam; the splash and giggle of him throwing in his duck; the sensation of my reddened hand swirling the squirt of baby soap through the water; all these soothed and smoothed the wrinkles of thought.

"Door. See. Lady. Door." A third time, I watched his round rosy cheeks, his bright eyes entranced, his little boy's hand held out. The wooden bannister, worn shiny by decades of steadying palms, bore no hand that I could discern. Finally, the chill in my bones and along my spine, I told him it was time for his bath.

"Say goodbye," I said.

"Bye bye." His reedy little voice piped out in the echoing space. He paused a moment and said it again, waving. He paused another moment and then smiled broadly, waving once more. On a whim, I spoke up too.

"Thank you for visiting." A sudden unexpected draught felt for all the world like a breath on my cheek and my neck prickled.

"Bath time," I said firmly and stepped back into the warmth of our flat. I closed the door and he was contented, slithering down to the varnished boards of the hallway. His lengthening legs pattered ahead of me, arms out to the side with forearms and hands raised up to the ceiling. Round bottom dancing, he glanced back to be sure I was following.

Just the two of us, now.

The Tibetan game of health and safety

Matt Wingett

It is true that Jack Mack could be a bit of a joker, but I've always believed in the perfectibility of people.

I can see him now, climbing that dizzying ladder on the crane to inspect the safety railings and flashing a full octave from his cheeky little face.

Jack knew me as a Buddhist, and that's why he used to rag me.

"I'm coming back as a psychopath," he would say. "But I'll only kill bad people. What will that do to my Karma, eh, Dolly the Llama?"

Since he asked, I called up to him and told him about Dhamma, Karma and the four noble truths as laid down in Buddhism. It would be untrue to say he didn't take any notice. Far from it. In fact, he leered, goading me I suppose.

Every Monday he would tell me all about his weekend adventures.

"Three in a bed," he would pronounce swaggering like a pirate, unbuttoning his shirt to show the scratch marks. Or: "What a fight. Silly sod didn't stand a chance," brandishing his dented knuckles.

To be honest he did seem a fish out water in Health and Safety. I suppose he used the weekend excitement to compensate for his weekday boredom.

One day he told me about a girl. Clever. Classy parents. Blondely pale. "In need of a man," so he claimed.

A glimmer came. "I'm going to give her merry hell, my Buddhist friend," he told me.

Once again I told him about reincarnation, and how the bad things we do are visited upon us in the Karmic cycle. We were doing a check on a gantry at the time. Swinging from the safety rail he laughed and called down to me:

"Karmic cycle?! How many miles to the litre, my friend?" Then he vanished into the sky to finish his safety check.

My Buddhism started when I was a boy.

Coming home from school to find my big brother sitting cross-legged and burning joss-sticks, I later realised I had caught him inthe twin acts of growing his hair and meditating.

After I'd clattered about our room for a bit my brother opened his eyes and glared.

"Do you ever think about reincarnation?" He asked, meaningfully.

Reincarnation. This was a new word.

"When you're dead, you get to come back as someone else," he explained.

"Why?" I asked.

"What?"

"Why? Why would you do that?"

He creased his brow and paused for a whole minute.

A few days after Jack Mack announced his blonde, he told me her name was Melissa. "She's 16, but looks younger," he said, excitedly. "Lovely. We met at Hammel's, on a machinery check."

Hammel's is the biscuit factory. They'd huddled over a cup of tea and he'd asked if he could dunk his chocolate finger. She'd blushed. He'd liked that.

"So fresh-faced," he said.

A few weeks after my brother explained reincarnation, a man on the telly told me about the work of Dr Duncan MacDougall who discovered that his dying patients lost an average 21 grams at the point of death. There could be no other explanation: 21 grams was the weight of the soul flying its cage. And if a soul left the body, it had to go somewhere. It suddenly made my brother's Buddhism plausible.

After we'd isolated the power at a power plant inspection, Jack Mack brushed carelessly by the ceramic insulation sheathing and called out to me. "She tells me she never had a dad. He pissed off when she was a kid." He looked up from scrutinising the ceramic surface for hairline cracks and winked at me. "Which wasn't that long ago."

I said to him levelly: "21 grams, my friend."

He put his hands up, palms outward, level with his shoulders in mock innocence, his eyebrows raised in a question, his mouth an O.

"I said I'd treat her right. That's what I'm doing. "

"Are you sure?"

"She's having fun. Going with an older man. Tomorrow we go out for coke. It's an adventure."

"Coca-Cola is an adventure?"

He belly laughed. "Not Coca-Cola. *Cocaine*, Buddha boy. *Cocaine!*"

I could hear his Karmic Wheel spinning like a Catherine Wheel.

After I asked my brother to tell me more about Buddhism, he lifted a board from a shelf and laid it on the floor.

"Let's play the Tibetan Game of Reincarnation," he said.

The board had a series of concentric circles and an enigmatic fat chap looking over it all. I loved the circles. There were counters - oh, and a big book, too.

He explained that in this ancient Tibetan game each throw of the dice stood for a life and a death, and how virtuously it was lived.

"So this is the game," my brother went on. "We all start off as ordinary people and we make mistakes or we do kindnesses. When we die, our 21 grams leave us and our souls go into something else."

He went on, speaking as if I were an idiot in the way older brothers do:

"Score high on the dice and you come back as a wealthier person, or a prince or someone essentially higher up, somehow. Throw a low number and you come back as a cat, a mouse or a buffalo. You look up the result in the book."

"Keep throwing low numbers and you keep going down. You might come back as a vegetable. A marrow or something even more rubbish. Like a pea. Or a lentil, even."

I didn't have time to question how a lentil might live a good or a bad life because, to be honest, I was on a roll, spiralling up through celestial circles - a higher form of life fast transforming into a bodhisattva. I just kept rising and rising.

Things weren't going so well for my brother. First he was a dog, then a flea on the dog, then a worm inside a dog's intestines. Soon he was in the outer circle of hell where his skin was flayed from him for ten thousand years. Next he was a parasite being passed through the back end of a demon for eons. A few more throws and he was trapped forever in the inner circle of hell. Completely irredeemable.

As for me, after a few more throws, I attained enlightenment. I had achieved Nirvana, in which all sense of self was lost. Like an overtopped pizza, I was *one with everything.*

"Shall we play again?" I blurted, hardly able to contain myself at this game of celestial snakes and ladders.

My brother was quiet for a few seconds.

"Nah, don't think so," he muttered. He gathered the game up and put it away.

He stopped being a Buddhist after that.

One morning Jack Mack came into the office without his customary grin.

"Sleepless night?" I asked. "Or not go to bed at all," I added, expecting the next instalment in the extended tale of debauchery that was his life.

"Woman trouble," he grunted, and made himself a thick cup of coffee in the office kitchen. He stared at the car park below, sunshine glimmering on puddles where a violent shower had just given the tarmac a hose down.

I waited, hoping he'd finally reached rock bottom. I was always charitable. If he just started being kind he might yet move up the ladder of reincarnation. Sometimes that's how Karma worked.

"Silly bitch has only gone and got herself knocked up," he said caustically. "I said to her, well what do you expect me to do about it?"

"And what did she say?"

"*Marry me.* I mean. Come on. It's the 21st Century. I told her, *I can't be having this.* I told her to get rid of it." He gulped his coffee down decisively. It was so hot it should have burned him. But that was him. He was fireproof, which is no bad thing for a Health and Safety man. Though, of course, he'd had an accident with his little girlfriend.

He started to walk past me and his eyes came level with mine. "I'm leaving her. Silly bitch can't stay off the white stuff, neither."

"Twenty one gra –" I started, but he put his finger on my lips, looked at me for two long seconds, patted my shoulder and walked away.

My Buddhism literally changed my life.

It made me do good things. I grew kinder. I had rituals for helping people, caring for people because that is what you do when you want to be perfect and you want others to be perfect.

I tried to explain it all to Jack Mack later that week. All about how it all comes back to you. Karma. The Wheel. How we are all perfectible. But Jack was speaking to me less and less, let alone listening.

One day he didn't come in to work at all. I learned what happened from the newspapers. She turned up at his house in the night, 4 months pregnant, banging on the door in the rain. There was a big argument and he told her to get lost.

The next day she went into work as usual and went down to look at the big industrial mixer. In interview with the police, Jack said that in the previous few weeks she'd asked him a lot of questions about how the mixer worked. Technical information that she'd said was all about wanting to be more than just the girl who loads biscuits on to warehouse pallets or polishes stainless steel.

Somehow, she'd managed to climb into the industrial mixer and bypass the safety circuits.

The coroner recorded a narrative verdict, unable to directly apportion blame. The papers of course knew differently, and Jack Mack appeared in the tabloids, distraught and contrite. He went through the whole process of repentance.

I thought, *well, maybe this time.*

He was suspended for a few months and then someone somewhere decided he could come back to work.

When he returned, the old sparkle had come back.

"I've met someone," he said. "So naive. I can't resist her." Then he held up his finger as I opened my mouth. "Don't you start. I looked up that thing about MacDougall, the doctor, you told me. There ain't no 21 grams. That's just made up."

That came as a shock that last thing he said. It made me think.

*

That was the last time I saw Jack Mack alive. At the inquiry, they said that what with the strain he'd been under, it was no surprise that when he went up on that gantry and leaned over the safety rail as he'd done a hundred times before, he didn't check that the fixings were secure.

Were unseen Karmic forces of retribution at work? Maybe. Maybe not. I can't say. You see, I'm not a Buddhist any more. Jack was right. Dr MacDougall's research was all wrong. There's no such thing as a soul.

I have always believed in the perfectibility of people. I used to think they just needed more time on this Earth and they would make the leap from this to the next stage of being.

That's why I became a Health and Safety officer. If I could just keep people safe, they would gain enlightenment.

I protected everyone. For ten years, I made sure that people could hardly move without tripping over safety equipment. It was a missionary zeal to keep people so safe they could hardly do a thing.

When Jack Mack dropped the bombshell that there was no 21 grams, I never wavered for a moment. Sure, there was no soul. But the species. The species could be perfected.

It's just a question of weeding out the wrong 'uns. It can be done quite easily. A twist of a safety railing's securing pin, the loosening of a safety rope, the forgetting to shut off the power to a circuit. It's all there, right before you.

The thing about Jack Mack's accident is you've got to see the bigger picture. It's not about the individual. It's the Health and Safety of the species. That's what really counts when you're looking for perfectibility.

Meek inheritance

A J Noon

Chris looked behind him to check he was still being followed. In the lengthening shadows cast by the tired tower blocks he could just make out the man who had been trailing him for the last fifteen minutes. The man moved slowly, almost shuffling, and every step looked to be causing him pain, but he was getting closer. With some impatience rising, Chris rang the doorbell twice more before knocking.

"Come on Nan, it's Chris." He called out, trying to sound casual as he could.

There was no answer and he could hear no sounds from inside the bungalow.

With another look over his shoulder he could see the figure had reached his side of the street, despite the half-limping, half-stumbling steps he took. It was not the first of them he had seen; over the last three weeks he had encountered, and easily avoided, more than a dozen of them. They were slow, and not very bright, they just made their way towards the nearest living person. The papers were reporting them as a nuisance more than a horror, which only fuelled Chris's belief it was a government cover-up. Porton Down, Gruinard, even Portsmouth University had been running tests. He had read about them all and the tests they had conducted over the last fifty years. He knew something must have been escaped. Or been released.

This morning though, when he had awoken to bright sunshine streaming through his bedroom window, he had had his idea. Not an overly complicated one, which was unusual for him, but one he was sure he could pull off. He just had to get into the bungalow first.

Chris balled his hand into a fist, ready to knock again, when he heard the chains being undone. He lowered his hand whilst the rattling continued and then finally the noises stopped and the door opened. In front of him, no more than five feet tall and with a quizzical look on her face, was the Mouth of Peckham, also known as his Nan.

"Chris? Is it Sunday?"

"No Nan, it's Wednesday, I thought I'd pop in and see you as I was passing," he checked behind him, "Come on and let's get in, stop letting all the heat out."

She did not move except to angle her head as she peered at him, "Are you okay? You look very flushed. Why are you sweating?"

"Come on Nan, let's get in."

Chris gently pushed his Nan back into the bungalow and towards the kitchen, "You get the kettle on and I'll get the door."

As she made her way out of the hall he made a pretence of locking the door, banging the chains against the metal but not securing them. He looked round to make sure she could not see then he slipped the latch on so the door would not lock.

The kettle was boiling and Nan was laying out a china plate with biscuits when he entered the cramped kitchen. They were his favourite chocolate bourbons he noted with a feeling of guilt. She put the plate in the centre of the table and waved for him to sit down.

"So why are you visiting today?" She eyed him suspiciously, "What are you after? I've no money you know."

"Nan! I told you, I was just passing. I thought I'd see if you needed anything."

"That I don't believe. You're thirty years old and unless it's the Sunday visit your mum makes you do, you've never been to see me without an ulterior motive." She paused to catch her breath, "And I still haven't got any money. Now stop loitering and sit down, we'll soon see what you're up to."

She pointed to one of the chairs by the table. They had vinyl covers with a red pattern that was now so faded it looked more like smudges of ketchup. Or blood, Chris thought morbidly.

She looked him over as he hovered by the seat, unwilling to place himself so near the door, "Well, have a biscuit at least, tea will brewed in a minute."

As Chris reached for one of the biscuits he heard a creak from the front door. He coughed loudly to cover the noise and then moved around the table to be as far from the door to the hall as he could. The cold handle of the fridge pressed into his back and he squirmed against it trying to make himself as unobtrusive as possible.

"So how are you Nan?" he asked, trying to keep her distracted.

"Since Sunday? What do you think has changed since then? Monday, breakfast porridge. Bingo, lost. Tuesday, breakfast porridge. Bingo, lost" She thought about it, and then remembered something else, "Though the Bridge club has been decimated by illness and we usually play today. An' I feed them, best bit of beef when I can get it. All of 'em caught it. Except me of course. You know I got that from the war, constitution of an ox and figure of a prima ballerina."

She gave Chris an arthritic twirl and he forced a smile in appreciation.

A floorboard in the hallway creaked. Nan stopped mid-spin and looked to the doorway.

"You did lock the door didn't you Chris?"

Chris nodded, but could not take his eyes from the doorway.

It was followed by a low groan and Nan picked up a saucepan, half-full of cold stew from the previous night.

"Right! I knew you were up to something. Have you let one of your pals in to rob me?"

Chris only managed a shake of his head.

"Well you won't mind if I call the Police then will you."

He shook his head, but realised he was holding a bourbon out in front of him as a weapon. He gingerly put the biscuit down onto the edge of the table.

A hand appeared in the doorway and gripped the wood. The fingers were covered in mud and, wrapped around the wrist, something he hoped was part of a string of sausages.

Nan took a step back, "Oh bugger, the phone's in the hall!" she looked about and saw the back door was ajar.

"I'm going to go through the garden to the living room, there's a phone a there. You keep him talking."

"Talking?" Before he could say more she shoved the saucepan

into Chris's hands and bolted out of the door. Despite the situation Chris was impressed by her speed; she seemed to have forgotten about her arthritis. And her prolapse. He dreaded to think what it was doing for her incontinence.

The sight of the shambling figure entering the kitchen stirred him and he threw the saucepan before turning and following Nan. His aim was poor though and the saucepan bounced off the light switch and onto the floor, leaving stew dripping down the wall.

Chris ran through the garden and into the living room, sliding the patio doors shut and locking them. His plan had fallen apart and he needed to turn this around. He took a step back before drawing the curtains tightly shut, another line of defence. He needed time to think.

"I don't think that'll stop 'em," said Nan.

He turned and in the dim light he could just make her out as she locked the door to the hallway.

"I'll do that Nan" he offered, stepping towards her.

"You must be joking! After you let that one in. What are you after? I told you I've no money. And give me the truth this time. I know when you're lying."

Chris took a breath, his heart was still racing and he could feel how flushed his face was. He looked his Nan in the eye and knew he could not lie to her again.

"It's the inheritance Nan. I thought if something happened to you I'd get my inheritance early. Me and Lou could get a place of our own then, you know how she is."

He looked down at the carpet, unable to meet her gaze.

She snorted then shook her head, "Hmmpf. Knew it was money you were after."

Chris looked up and realised he could see more of the room now his eyes had adjusted to the gloom. There were figures on the sofa.

"Who are they?"

"It's the Bridge Club. I told you we meet on a Wednesday."

"But you said they were ill?"

"Oh, they are. I didn't say what with though did I?"

The shapes slowly stood up, more elderly blighted by arthritis Chris thought at first, and he counted seven of them.

His Nan edged away from him, "Now they have a nice place to

stay here with me and they don't want their routine to be upset."

"What do you mean? Upset?"

"You Chris. You've upset their routine. You shouldn't be here on a Wednesday, and you shouldn't be wanting me dead."

The figures started to enclose Chris and before he could react his Nan slipped out through the door. A hand gripped his wrist, it was cold and clammy. Low moans emanated from cracked lips and he could feel teeth bearing down on his shoulder.

As she locked the door his Nan called out to him, "And I told you, I always lay on food for the Bridge Club."

Neighbourhood watching

Tom Pinnock

It all began I suppose when that dreary old fool next door to me, Terry Evans, went and kicked the bucket - Leaving his cottage empty.

It was a Wednesday in early June and I'd risen late. Not at all like me, but a bad habit I'd got into and one I couldn't seem to shift for love nor money. I pulled back my bedroom curtains and happened to glance into next door's garden. There she was again, just like every other morning – The great lady I am, Sally Jones.

I couldn't stick the sight of her. I know it wasn't very neighbourly of me, but that's how I felt. There was just something about her that put my hackles up. Every morning it was the same. She'd swan off down the garden path in that hat, those big gloves and carrying the garden trowel like she was the Queen of Sheba.

She hadn't long moved in, but she'd already ingratiated herself in the village.

Even Deidre Smith from opposite, who had until recently been quite a bosom pal of mine, seemed to be completely under her spell. "She's a very pleasant woman, Mrs Weaver," she said to me. "If a bit fancy. She's from the posh part of London. Very charming." She says. She certainly didn't charm me.

So, as I'd done countless times before, I dashed downstairs and crept out the back door. Edging alongside the hedge which bordered both our gardens, I watched as she tended her flock. It's ridiculous I know, a woman of my age, reduced to hiding in the bushes in her nightie and spying on the neighbours, but you see... she was hiding something, and I knew it. She crouched there digging around her plants, pulling up weeds like nobody's business. All around her, a sweet-sickly smell permeated the air. It made me feel quite ill.

I tried to tell myself I'd gone bananas on account of being left all alone in the cottage after Arthur had passed on. He'd never have stood for all this.

I just couldn't stand the sight of her, floating about her dahlias, cooing at them gently.

So, there I was, watching the next door neighbour, when I suddenly thought - Am I going mad? Crouching in the garden, in my night things, watching Sally Jones dig up her garden? Oh, but I knew she was up to something. And I seemed to be the only one who realised it.

The days passed almost normally for a little while.

It had been an early summer, and the village of Stourbridge was basking in the heat. The villagers put on their shorts and summer dresses. At least the ladies did. I was too worried about what Sally Jones was up to.

One day, I just had to get out of the house, but it was then I unfortunately bumped into the Vicar.

"Ah, there you are Mrs Weaver, popping out for some provisions are you?"

"Afternoon Reverend Jones. I'm just in need of some scouring pads."

I knew that wouldn't placate him.

"We don't seem to see you around the village as much as we used to?"

I told him I liked to keep myself to myself and what not. Then he started on about the sterling work my new neighbour was doing for the upcoming Stockbridge Summer Flower fair. I just couldn't help myself.

"Oh dear, you're not going to bring this up again are you?"

"I can't be the only one in the village who thinks she's a little bit suspect?"

"Suspect! Mrs Weaver, she's a charming woman. I'm quite looking forward to her promised Dahlia display. I think she's a delightful person."

I stared at him for a second, before trying a different tack.

"She's got you all wrapped around her little finger, hasn't she?!

The whole bally lot of you!"

"Mrs Weaver I really can't see how -"

"I've had enough of this. If you can't see through her veneer of charm, then I just despair Vicar! I really do! That woman is evil I tell you!"

"Evil? Oh really"

"I don't use that word lightly."

"I think you better go home and calm yourself. Have a lie down with a cold compress. Put your feet up."

"I can see there's no point in talking about this with you!"

"Good day, Mrs Weaver"

I bustled home, livid. How dare he talk to me like that! How dare he not take seriously the fears of one of his parishioners!

I made myself some tea, and sat stiffly at the kitchen table bristling with fury. Out of the back window I could see next door's garden. Sure enough, there was the elegant and unruffled Sally Jones, wending her way through her Hollyhocks. I thought to myself, could I be going mad? Why was I so fixated on this newcomer to Stockbridge? Perhaps I just didn't have enough to keep my mind occupied?

Then a very odd thing happened.

In the middle of the night I awoke with a start. There were noises. Someone was moving about outside. I knew instantly who it would be. I threw on my dressing gown, the nice Chinese one that Arthur had brought me back from his travels, and crept down to investigate.

It was a clear, cool moon-lit night, but there she was – Gardening again. The smell around her Dahlias was stronger, sort of sweet, but rank also. In the light I could just make out why. She was pouring some sort of strange concoction onto the roots. A dark, hot, steaming brew – And I hate to say it, but it looked like blood!

I sat there transfixed, and it took her a matter of moments as she finished soaking her Dahlias. Then she tottled off back into her cottage, bold as brass.

She still had that old fool Evan's composter down at the end of her garden, and that's where the hedge is the thinnest. I had to know what she was up to, so I pushed through, sneaked up the garden path and crept into the bright kitchen.

The kitchen was transformed from how old Evans had it, all new and polished, yellow flowers and cutesy bric-a-brac everywhere.

Nestling on the Aga was another one of her horrid concoctions, bubbling away and spewing its disgusting stench into the room.

"One of my mother's old recipes." Sally said from the doorway. She had the trowel dangling from her finger tips, as she leaned in the door frame. "It's made from fish, blood and bone, and a few additives. She was a wonderful cook, but also a superb maker of liquid fertiliser."

I was right! I picked up the pan and sniffed it suspiciously.

"Whose bone? Whose blood?"

"Don't be silly Mrs Weaver, it's just store bought! From that place on the high street."

"You expect me to believe that? And why the middle of the night?"

"All the better to hide it away from prying eyes. I've seen you watching me. Trying to pick up tips were you?"

Well, that really infuriated me. Imagine her thinking I was copying her! Of all the things I'd done, I could safely say I could handle growing plants all on my own, thank you very much!

I waved the pan at her, its contents splashing about on the kitchen floor.

"You think I need gardening tips from the likes of you? How dare you!"

She came in and put the trowel on the table.

"Now, now Mrs Weaver, you're just a silly old woman. Come on, we need to get you back to bed."

She stepped towards me, and that's when it happened. All that stupid soup on the floor, she didn't stand a chance.

She fell backwards, arse over tit and with a loud crack, high and mighty Sally Jones smacked her head on the hearth.

Her body lay there, staring at the ceiling. But not at me. I was too busy climbing back through the hedge.

Any road, the funeral was a solemn affair, with some of Sally's highfalutin London friends, down for a good old weeping. It didn't take long.

I hadn't planned on going to the wake, but I decided at the last minute to pop in to the village hall and pay my respects. See what the sandwiches were like.

The vicar was standing by the food table, his duties all over with - He was taking his time with some canapés.

He glanced up as I approached.

"Oh I do hope you're feeling all right, Vicar?"

"Yes, Mrs Weaver. It's such a shame, to see someone so young pass over."

"She was a lovely woman Vicar, I always said so."

He looked at me, for a second.

"Really Mrs Weaver? I got the distinct impression you weren't keen on Miss Jones?"

"Oh no, as I say, I was coming around to her. She was a wonderful woman."

"Really? You told me she was -"

"Anyway, it looks like there might not be much competition in this year's Summer Flower Fair? Now that Sally won't be displaying her Dahlias."

He stood up, looking at me quite funny.

"This is true, Mrs Weaver. And of course last year with Mister Evans passing, meant we didn't have his award winning Roses. It's all been a rather harrowing time."

"Yes, that was one of things I advised her when she moved in, 'You better get those stair rods fixed!' I told her. It was such a shame about his accident."

It was then I saw Deidre Smith, and hurried off to discuss the horrendous potholes in the road outside her house.

Maybe in the New Year, I'll have to do something about that Vicar?

The guide

James Bicheno

'Woah, now! Careful there, sir,' Christopher heard the man's voice echo around the tower's stone walls as he crashed into him. 'You'll smash your head on them walls if you're not careful.'

'Sure. Right,' Christopher said as he straightened up, catching his breath in the cold air. 'Thank you. Thank you very much.'

'Are you all right?' the man asked. Christopher saw the uniform, he was a tour guide.

'Oh yes,' Christopher said. 'Lost my footing on the steps.'

'That's the problem with these listed buildings, sir,' the guide said. 'They can only do so much to make 'em safe.'

'Indeed,' Christopher said, dusting himself down.

'Now, begging your pardon sir, but I thought I'd locked all the rooms on that level. Did I miss one?'

'Oh, I can't say I saw you,' Christopher replied, evading the question.

'Well, sir, I'm afraid the tower is closed for visitors now,' the guide shot him a quizzical glance as he strode over to lock another door. 'Sorry for the inconvenience. Rules are rules, so if you'd care to follow me...'

'Actually,' Christopher said, realising he had to come clean. 'Well, actually I was hiding upstairs, hoping everyone had gone.'

'I'm sorry?' the guide raised an eyebrow. Christopher noticed he was a touch pale, probably having to work long hours in such a cold, damp environment.

'I must confess I snuck in as the staff at the ticket office were cashing up. Once inside I crept upstairs and hid. I thought everyone had gone.'

'Did you now, sir?' the guide asked, his voice taking on the tone of a zealous policeman.

'Yes,' Christopher said, head bowed, not wanting to meet the older fellow's eye.

'So you dodged the ticket office, then?' the guide asked, taking a notebook and pen from his pocket.

'Yes but I...'

'I will need to take your name and address, sir,' the guide turned to a clean page. 'And you are?'

'Look,' Christopher said, holding his hands up. 'I left a five pound note at the entrance. You'll see it on the way out.'

'Really?' the guide asked.

'Yes, look I'm here because I want to...' he tried to order his thoughts to make his case convincing. 'Well, I want to stay here. Overnight.'

'Out of the question I'm afraid, sir,' the guide said with a shake of the head. 'The tower must be cleared of people before I leave. You'll put my job on the line, see?'

'But can't you just pretend you haven't seen me?' Christopher asked. 'Plead innocence?'

The guard shook his head.

'I'll hide somewhere while the staff open up tomorrow morning and sneak out while no one's watching. After all, a tower like this is bound to have all kinds of hiding places.'

'Ha, ha, I'll be hauled over coals for not checking properly as I locked up. No, I'm afraid you'll have to come with me, sir and sort something out with the managers in the morning.'

'Look,' Christopher said, stopping the guide. 'I just need to spend one night here. Or at least let me accompany you on your rounds as you lock up.'

'Well...' the guide looked unsure.

Christopher took his wallet from inside his jacket. 'I can pay you.'

'You trying to bribe me, sir?' the guide raised an eyebrow.

'No, I will be paying you for a service. A private tour, if you like. Once you've finished locking up I'll leave with you. No one stays overnight, no rules broken and no one needs to know about it. Shall we say ten pounds?'

'Twenty.'

'What?' Christopher's eyes widened.

'It is my job at risk, sir,' the guide shrugged and a smiled.

'Fifteen?' Christopher offered.

'Seventeen...' the guide said.

'Done,' Christopher held out a hand in triumph.

'Pounds fifty,' the guide finished.

'What?' Christopher snatched his hand away as the guide began to take it.

'Seventeen pounds and fifty in the Her Majesty's coin, if you please. In exchange for the grand tour of this vintage building, complete with jangling keys,' the guide added, rattling the large set of keys at the end of a chain.

'Oh very well,' they shook on the deal and the money changed hands.

'So,' the guide began as he paced around the main chamber, stuffing his bonus into a pocket. 'What's so special about this place you're willing to hide away in the shadows for a night?'

'Well, the thing is,' Christopher said, following him. 'I'm a journalist. Freelance. Work's a bit tight so I'm writing a few pieces on local legends in the hope of attracting one of the local papers.'

'Legends eh?' the guide repeated with a raised eyebrow.

'Yes,' Christopher answered, as his enthusiasm rose. 'And from what I hear this tower has its fair share of stories to tell.'

'In other words you're one of them ghost hunters,' the guide said, rolling his eyes.

'You've had a few then?' Christopher said with a laugh.

'You could say that.'

'Well, Most Haunted is rather popular these days.'

'You what?' the guide looked puzzled.

'Most Haunted? You know, that show where paranormal investigators visit haunted locations?'

'No. Never heard of it,' the guide shook his head. 'Don't really watch much telly, to be honest.'

'Not even the episode they filmed here, a few months ago?'

'No. No one said nothing. Must have been off that week.'

'Right,' Christopher shrugged.

'So,' the guide said. 'What's made you take up ghost-busting?'

'Well it's something people like to read and hear about. Especially around Christmas and Halloween. Plenty of money to be made from it.'

'Indeed there is, sir,' the guide patted his pocket with a smile. 'So, did those people on that Haunted programme find anything?'

'Well, they came to find ghosts. They didn't. But so many people claim to have seen them.'

'Is that right?'

'What about yourself? Have you seen any?'

'Well...' the guide pondered. 'There have been times, certain nights, when I thought I'd seen things. Sometimes... heard them but...'

'Yes?' Christopher had his pen at the ready.

'No,' the guide shook his head as if to rid himself of some ridiculous notion. 'No.'

'What did you hear or see - or you think you heard or saw?'

The guide pondered for a moment.

'It could just be my mind playing tricks on me, or just from hearing other people but...'

'Yes?' Christopher's eyes widened in hope.

'Well, on some nights, in certain lights, I sometimes see a soldier. Like something from Napoleon's time. Up there, walking about. His footsteps echoing above,' he shone his torch up to a balcony on the next level. 'And there are times, if you look to what's left of the church outside,' he shone his torch out of the window, 'you can see a monk or a nun walking up some invisible steps where there used to be a staircase.'

'Fascinating,' Christopher said, pen scrawling each word down in frantic detail.

'And sometimes, if you go to the very top, though I don't do that so often now, you can just about make out a Roman soldier. This tower used to be a Roman fort in its earliest times, you see.'

'Ah yes, I've heard of that,' Christopher said. 'But sightings of him have been very rare, I heard.'

'I might have only seen him a couple of times. Very faint. Almost as if he was half in and half out of the wall. But let's not forget, the Medieval tower, that we are standing in, was built on top of the Roman foundations.'

'Well indeed. They probably built right on top of the poor ghost.' Christopher said with a laugh.

'So what do you make of those, then?' the guide asked. 'Scary enough for you?'

'Well I wouldn't go as far as to say scary,' Christopher said. 'Does the soldier say or do anything?'

'Don't think so. I've probably seen him three, maybe four times. He just walks up and down. I don't think he's noticed me.'

'Well, if that's the case then we've nothing to fear.'

'Oh yeah?' the guide asked in a doubtful tone. 'Why's that then?'

'Well, I've read about this sort of thing. A ghost, as we call them, is sometimes believed to be the energy left behind when someone dies. Perhaps they were in the prime of their life or if they died violently or without knowing - in any case, they were not ready to pass to the other side. So they just keep on as if nothing's any different. Perhaps our friends here were killed by an accident, or by war?'

'Right.'

'Anyhow, in the case of these historical figures, the energy fades over time. Think of them as old films or photographs. You say the soldier walks about. Do you hear noises? See colours?'

'A little, I think. Very faint, though.'

'Well that's it. It's like a worn out video. The sounds and picture have faded over time. The monk or nun sounds like a silent film that just has them walking up stairs. As for your Roman friend up there, you say he just stands around?'

'Yeah. Like a photo.'

'Well that's exactly that. The energy has worn away over the centuries. All that remains is his image and that's only when the moonlight and clouds are at a certain strength and distance.'

'Blimey!' the guide said with a laugh. 'So it takes over two thousand years for them to pass over.'

'That's what they say,' Christopher answered, remembering the research he'd done. 'Though, it is said we can help them along to the afterlife - whatever the afterlife might be.'

'Sort of – go to the light?' the guide asked, waving the torch and laughing a little at the idea.

'Yes, although I think they'll be needing something more substantial,' Christopher answered. 'A lit room is best, so I hear, or several candles. But you wouldn't really want to deprive your visitors of this entertainment, would you? It'd mean a huge drop in income for the place!'

'It might do. But, as you may know from your reading into such things, legends live on. We could set these ghosts free and no one need know about it. They never appeared on the telly, well it's not stopped people – like you - coming here, has it?'

'True,' Christopher nodded.

'And we'd be putting these poor souls to rest. I don't know about you, sir, but it does seem a bit Mediaeval to be making entertainment out of their plight.'

'I suppose you're right,' Christopher said. 'Although a bit apt given we're in a Medieval tower. Are there any rooms with emergency lighting?'

'The other chamber next door, now you come to mention it,' the guide said, walking to a corner and flicking a switch. The second room filled with light. A big green EMERGENCY EXIT sign lit up above the door. 'There we go. Quite apt, really.'

Both stood, waiting.

'What happens, then?' the guide whispered. 'Do we go and call for them?'

'They should arrive of their own accord,' Christopher said.

The guide thought for a moment. 'You know, I'm not sure I'm all that happy about this.'

'Oh really?' Christopher asked. 'Why not?'

'Well, telling people to leave this way. Doesn't feel right,' the guide's face was lined with concern.

'Would you prefer it if we had a priest present or some other minister?'

'No, it's just when I show people round they always leave through the gift shop!' the guide wheezed a laughed, slapping Christopher on the shoulder.

'Oh really,' Christopher shook his head disapprovingly, but secretly grateful for the humour.

'I'm sorry, sir, I didn't mean to ruin your experiment,' the guide said, laughter ebbing. 'You know, it feels a bit odd in here, now, don't you think?'

'Yes it does,' Christopher said as he hugged his coat around himself. 'The temperature has definitely dropped.'

The guide tensed. 'Can you hear that?'

'Hear what?' Christopher listened out.

'Shh!' he waved for quiet. 'That tapping,' he whispered.

Christopher could make out light tapping, almost like footsteps. They moved, echoing down the stone stairs and then onto the floor. In the moonlight Christopher gasped as the faint coloured outline of a British redcoat soldier moved slowly but surely towards the light in the room. The face was a young man but marked with scars, either from war, disease or both. He walked with a slight limp.

'Go,' Christopher whispered. 'Go inside. You'll find peace there.'

If the figure was aware of what Christopher was saying or even if he knew the two men were there, he did not give any sign. He simply walked inside, drawn to the light as if by instinct. The glow gathered around him, causing him to fade away.

Neither the guide nor Christopher spoke for some time.

'Well,' Christopher said, throat dry. 'Seems it does work.'

'Look,' the guide said and pointed.

At the doorway to the chamber stretched the moonlight shadow of a hooded figure.

'The monk,' he whispered.

'Or nun,' the guide said.

Almost on cue, the hooded figure half walked, half hovered towards the light. Not paying any attention to Christopher or the guide, the figure entered the room, again fading away.

'Now for the Roman,' the guide said. 'Do you think he'll be aware?'

'I hope so,' Christopher said. 'Although his energy may not be strong enough. You saw how slow the monk was...'

'Or nun,' the guide added.

'Yes, or nun,' Christopher waved his hand. 'But you saw how slow he or she was compared to the soldier. I wondered if they would ever get there at all.'

'I'll keep the light on each night,' the guide said. 'If that doesn't work I'll light some candles on the tower. Or a torch. Hopefully that'll work.'

'Indeed,' Christopher said. 'Now we just need to wait for the poltergeist.'

'The what?' the guide asked.

'The poltergeist you've got here,' Christopher said. 'I'm surprised you didn't mention him.'

'Can't say I know about that,' the guide shook his head.

'Well a poltergeist is a spirit, usually one who hasn't died that long ago, who leaves so much energy behind they can interact with the human world to some degree, unlike the others who can only just appear or repeat certain movements and sounds.'

'Yeah I know, I've seen the film. And we've got one of those here, you say?' the guide asked.

'Did no one tell you?' Christopher looked amused at the guide's incredulous look.

'Well no. No trees have tried to snatch me away and, as far as I know, this wasn't built on some burial ground.'

'It's the ghost of one of your predecessors.'

'What?'

'There was a guide about fifteen, twenty years ago who died of a heart attack when the tower was broken into one night. His keys can sometimes be heard jangling.'

'What?' the guide's face went white.

'Some youths scared the poor man to death it seemed. Didn't anyone tell you?'

'Look, I've been here as long as I remember. The only time I've ever had trouble was when I chased some kids away. Had a bit of tightness round my chest but...'

Both men looked at each other, both faces lost colour. Steam rose from their breaths in the cold, damp air.

'So I must be...' the guide said at last.

'So it seems,' Christopher's mouth had dried and his voice was nothing but a whisper as cracked as his throat.

'But how...?'

'There's only one way to be sure,' Christopher said, clearing his throat. 'Go inside. If you are that man you'll pass on. If not you can come back and we'll have a laugh at all this.'

The guide stepped very slowly to the room. Pausing at the entrance, he looked to Christopher.

'Go on,' he said. He saw the guide step in and the light wrapped its peaceful glow around him. The guide faded away.

'Oh my good God,' Christopher said, in a trembling voice. As a chill passed through him, he noticed what he thought was a Roman helmet pass into the light. The room suddenly felt almost warm.

Gathering what little courage remained, he went back toward the stairs where the guide had caught him. He had left his bag upstairs, with sandwiches and a flask of tea. He could do with that cuppa, right now.

'Well,' he said to himself, trying to calm his nerves. 'Seems I've had my life saved by a poltergeist.' He went to climb the stairs when he tripped and stopped, gaping in horror at what he saw. The moonlight shone down on an all too familiar body, only recently deceased, blood leaking from his head.

'Or have I?' Christopher asked in a shaking voice as he recognised the white face as his own.

He turned back and stepped into the room with its EMERGENCY EXIT sign above.

As the glow of the light embraced him, he felt a warm sense of peace.

Irukandji roulette

Tessa Ditner

She was making lamingtons, knew the recipe by heart, like a proper Ozzie. They'd run out of chocolate, so she went onto the deck, climbed down into the lifeboat and drove it along the narrow passage between the yachts and monstrously big Great Barrier Reef catamarans.

It was on the way back from the shops, as she stepped from the lifeboat up onto their sailing boat that her foot slipped. Her sandaled foot was submerged in the water for a moment, but it was the wrong moment. A sharp jab, the shopping scattered across the deck. Barely a mark on her ankle, despite the burn. Maybe the arthritis flaring up? She tidied up her mess. The jam jar had survived her clumsiness, raspberry, Bill's favourite. She got back to baking: melted the chocolate, dipped the squares of sponge in, one side, then the other. It was then, as she sprinkled coconut shavings into a bowl, daydreaming about DHL-ing a batch to the grandkids in England, that the sting took effect.

Bill heard the clatter of crockery, and swearing. He stuck his head through the door and made a quip about it. She tried to laugh, they'd been married 47 years, their sense of humour had long jelled, but her voice was muffled by the muscle cramps in her arms and legs.

Then her kidneys and back were wrung with pain and her face burnt up. She looked at the stove, but it was off. The burning was inside her. Bill called mayday on the radio and for an ambulance on their shared mobile phone. She made it as far as the hospital, pain despite the morphine, and then her body looked at her across the other side of a table. She burnt and shivered in the hospital bed. Her body sat quietly, leaned in and said: 'We've had a good life you and me.' Bill, on the chair beside her, his terrified face. 'He'll understand,' her body placed old, blue veined hands on the table. A click in her head and Bill melted into the walls.

Now. After. Bill sat at the back of their sailboat, the midday sun burning into his skin, the cat meowing for food. Skin cancer would take too long, he didn't want to sit like this, stupefied, he wanted justice for Jenny. But how do you take revenge on a fish? And this wasn't a Moby Dick sea monster, a thing with a brain, with intention or a sense of self-worth. Irukandjis are the world's most poisonous box jelly fish. The creature that killed the love of his life, was the size and appearance of a contact lens.

Bill stared up at the estuary, trying to spot their translucent bodies being washed down the river into the sea. He'd have welcomed a sighting of old Devil, the crocodile who roamed these waters. Crocs ate jelly fish, right? Old devil could eat anything. He'd tried to eat the captain of the prawn fishery, but the captain had thrown in his dog and saved himself. Since then, all the sailboats moored up in the cheap mooring spots, where old Devil liked to hunt, had purchased a pet just in case.

Jenny and Bill's cat hadn't been bought for old Devil. Jenny had rescued the emaciated fur ball from a beach in Papa New Guinea. It now meowed and licked the lamington bowl that had long been licked clean. The cat gazed out across the water at the yachts. Those posh pets were a hop away from a world of discarded prawn heads and barramundi tails. That's it, Bill thought, watching the cat watch the water. A jellyfish that firebombs your nervous system with your own hormones has no weapon of its own. The battleground is inside you. A fair fight, that's all he wanted. And if he lost, he would be eating lamingtons in the sky with Jenny.

First he fashioned a harness for the cat, with a long rod so she could stay out of the water. That way, he could yank her in if old Devil came sniffing, the decoy buying him enough time to climb back on board. A fair fight. Irukandji vs Bill. He stripped, maximum skin exposure, so the jelly fish had more chance of brushing him as they floated out to sea. Fired up by his plan, he felt a sense of elation. The cat tried to undo the harness with her claws, sensing things were not in her favour. Bill stood in waist height water for five minutes, then ten, where were they? A boat of tourists passed, they stared, the tour guide made up a story so as not to alarm them.

"That's Bill, he is wearing a flesh-coloured stinger suit," he lied.

"It's very realistic," a woman observed, "It even has chest hair!"

"But what about the crocs?" A kid asked pointing at the cat on the boat with a fishing rod attached. "And why is he fishing that cat?" The tour guide didn't have a clue why old Bill had attached a fishing rod to his cat. He sensed there might be some logic to it, there had been a spotting of a four metre saltie nearby.

"Haven't you seen Crocodile Dundee?" He improvised. "That movie was inspired by Bill." Then he radioed the Port Douglas police and told them the truth. Old Bill was mad with grief. He was starkers in the estuary, freaking out tourists. Within a few minutes a sleek blue vessel approached.

"Come on," three officers reasoned. They flexed their arms, the word POLICE on their ironed shirts. "Go swim up on the beach, inside the stinger nets. This is right where the young ones get washed out to sea after the first rains."

Bill hated the reminder. He splashed at them with the hand that wasn't holding onto the rod. The boat circled, trying to talk sense into the old fool. They couldn't arrest someone for going for an ill advised swim, and yet, letting him get stung or eaten didn't fill them with joy. The beaches might have to be closed, the lifeguards would be out of a job for the season, and there would be paperwork.

They tried to talk sense into him for 15 minutes. And then, finally, he felt it, the sting of the irukandji. He played compliant so they wouldn't ship him off to A&E. He thanked them for their lecture, promised he'd invest in a stinger suit. He climbed back into his home, flashing his naked butt at them, fetched a can of consolatory tuna for the cat and waved the police boat away, all gritted smiles. Then he lay on their bed. The bed he'd shared with Jenny for all these years as they had sailed, slowly, around the world. And the venom slid through his nerves and into his adrenal gland, where it released his hormones. His body fireworked with pain. He thought of Jenny, the way the hospital ward had gone quiet around them as her sweat-drenched face looked up at him for the last time.

His laughter was heard by the diners at the yacht club, deranged laughter that reached the congregation at St Mary's By The Sea. But the next day, Bill and the cat were gone.

Maybe he made it to England to cook Jenny's lamingtons for the grandkids. Maybe old Devil got them. But whenever the rains come, you can hear laughter in the mangroves, as if he's still there, naked in the water, winning, over and over at irukandji roulette.

The case of the Serbian dwarf poisoner

Matt Wingett

"Observe the way in which the victim is holding the napkin, Jenkins," said The Legend, drawing on his meerschaum as they stood over a corpse that lay sprawled in a grime-filled alley half-lit by the lambent glow of gaslight. "What does it tell you?"

Sergeant Jenkins turned his dull brown eyes toward his senior officer, his internal blankness seeping out across his face.

"That he wanted to wipe his mouth, Sir?" said the other, sighing. He was painfully aware of being in the presence of Portsmouth Constabulary's finest. A man of infinite imagination, who knew exactly how to piece together the evidence to create what he valued most: The Incriminating Narrative.

The Legend smiled superciliously as he peered at the napkin.

"Really Jenkins, have you learned nothing from your time with me?" he asked in that superior way, adding insult to injury by jabbing him rhythmically in the ribs with his pipe-stalk in time with his words. "Here we stand at the start of the 20th Century, and still your mind remains unreceptive to the sensitivities of my Narrative Method."

The skin around Sergeant Jenkins's eyes turned puce as he considered those final words uneasily.

The Narrative Method.

With it, The Legend claimed to have solved the most baffling crimes. For example, The Case of the Disappearing Dockyard Donkey.

That had been last year. The creature in question had just been loaded with the paymaster's strongbox, prior to disbursement to the crew of HMS Connaught, a ship newly docked, when it had disappeared without trace.

The Legend had demonstrated, through the construction of an elaborate narrative, that its disappearance had been initiated by a gentleman with a hare lip, angered at his rejection by society. This hare-lipped gentleman had arranged a meeting with a one-legged red-haired Russian, the pair concocting a plan that had somehow involved the Donkey's abduction. It was an undeniable fact, The Legend had insisted, that the loss of the strongbox was a diversion. Their true interest had indeed been the donkey...

"Or something," Sergeant Jenkins thought, his brow creasing to a distressed furrow as he tried to remember the tortuous narrative The Legend had devised to explain the Dockyard Donkey's Disappearance.

The case had caused a sensation in the Portsmouth Times, and The Legend had taken great pleasure in declaring to its editor his famous dictum:

"The Narrative Method is that by which the investigator weaves strands of gossamer to produce a web in which the villain is captured more surely than any spider apprehends its fly."

The hare-lipped Donkey thief and Russian monopod had spirited the creature away at night by hot air balloon, The Legend had explained. Enquiries through his secret network of helpers showed the co-conspirators to be living beyond the British Empire's jurisdiction, somewhere in Northern France. The Donkey's whereabouts and the nefarious uses it had been put to remained a mystery.

The case had filled many a column-inch and many an advertiser had advertised because of it. Indeed the Paymaster had become something of a minor celebrity as the victim of such a bizarre crime. So, when a few weeks later, Sergeant Jenkins spotted the submerged undersides of four hooves pointed at the sky, and beneath that the bloated corpse of a donkey, right near to where the Disappearing Donkey had vanished, it was declared by all parties concerned that this donkey was not *the* Donkey, but another donkey – in fact, an Appeared one.

Investigation had shown that this donkey had most likely fallen off the wharf in the night.

"Upon a barrowload of bibles, I've never seen *that* donkey before in my life," the Paymaster declared with the fervour of one perhaps apprehensive at losing not only his credibility but his Liberty. "I never tied the strongbox on *that* donkey's back, not never," he added, which raised all sorts of further questions.

In the ensuing moments in which suspicion took wing and neatly alighted on the Paymaster's shoulder like the heavy hand of the law, The Legend stepped in, looking down at the inverted creature in the murky depths.

"This definitely isn't the Donkey. *Obviously*," The Legend pronounced, his superior tone quelling all dissent, and giving the Paymaster a reassuring nod. "Observe the shape of the hooves..." he began, at which point Sergeant Jenkins went into something of a daydream.

So, with the solving of one mystery - that of the Disappearing Donkey - another was born. Not that The Legend was remotely interested in it. The Appearing Donkey's manifestation remained an unsolved mystery. The very afternoon of its discovery, The Legend refused to investigate further. After leaving the Paymaster's premises and putting down a deposit on a new house in the smarter end of town, he told Jenkins:

"*Disappearances,* these are matters for the force, Jenkins. But what is one to do with *appearances?*"

"Keep them up, Sir?" Jenkins had replied with rare wit, only to be ignored by The Legend, who nonetheless later that day used the very same line with the Lord Mayor, to much hilarity.

Now, standing in the alleyway over the body, Sergeant Jenkins huffed as he remembered the Donkey case. With a sinking feeling, he realised he was going to be forced to have another crack at the Narrative Method, which he always seemed to get wrong.

He suspected this was because his own father had been a man of little imagination.

"You've read one book, you've read them all," the Old Man once told him. Taking him at his word, Jenkins had decided to read them all; Charles Dickens's *Hard Times* being the one he chose. Gradgrind, that humourless individual who knew the danger of imagination was the character he most identified with.

Asked his opinion of Dickens's book by The Legend, Jenkins had replied: "Mercifully short, Sir." At the same time, he was pleased he had mastered all of English Literature in such a brief span.

As he was bid, Jenkins stepped up to the body and studied closely the napkin it still clutched. There was a crumb upon it, and a little smear of grease, along with the faint smell of stale beer.

He looked along the street. The body was not three hundred yards from The Mystery - a public house of dubious reputation. There was a deep dent in the top of the man's skull where someone had stoved in his brains.

In a flash, he saw a sequence of images moving in his mind like a play. Was this the elusive Narrative Method The Legend so oft quoted? He decided to unfold his story to The Legend and see what he thought.

"Well, the way I see it, Sir... um... bear with me," he straightened and cleared his throat. "H-hm. The unidentified man having had a beer and perhaps..." He knelt again and sniffed at the man's greasy fingers. "Perhaps a lamb chop smothered in gravy, wandered out here in the night, where he was set upon by an assailant or assailants unknown, using -" he leapt across the path to a pile of discarded newspapers in a corner of the alley and drawing a pen from out of his pocket, inserted it into the neck of a heavy stoneware bottle protruding from the pile. "Yes - using this empty blood-smeared ginger beer bottle as a weapon, Sir!" Jenkins announced, with genuine pride. He lifted it victoriously. On one side it was spattered with a crusted, sticky substance darkening to black, but still showing its original colour - blood red. "Now, Sir, how's that?"

The Legend drew himself to his full height and looked down on his short, stocky, bewhiskered Sergeant, his expression difficult to divine. He kept his narrowed eyes on Jenkins for a few moments longer as he considered the scenario he'd presented.

"Excellent. Excellent, Jenkins," he said with a flat, ironic tone, then followed his words with a slow hand clap. Jenkins stiffened. Were the slapping of those bony palms not enough to go on, the tone of voice told him what was coming next. It was the tone that preceded the one word he found the most infuriating whenever it issued from The Legend's lips. That word was -

"*However* - there are one or two things you appear to have overlooked."

"Sir?" said the Sergeant, a sinking feeling taking hold of him again. "Really Sir?"

"Indeed. You will recall, Jenkins, that I asked you to inspect the napkin still clasped in the dead man's hands. You will notice by the way it is folded that it was prepared for the table by a left-handed person. I wrote a monogram on the folding of napkins by left-handed people, and this fold conforms exactly to the Belgrade Variation. Furthermore, the angle at which pressure was applied to the napkin and the nature of the fold reveals a person of diminutive stature."

"Diminutive stature, Sir?"

"Correct, Jenkins. Now observe the twisted lip this man has developed. " (Jenkins could see nothing unusual about the lip.) "A sure sign of snake venom. The man who poisoned the unfortunate victim used a venom drawn from the fangs of the krait, the world's most deadly of snakes, thus revealing that the murderer has spent years in the subcontinent of India. In sum, we are seeking a left-handed travelling Serbian dwarf well versed in the art of poisoning. I believe that if you search the local hostelries -" he broke off for a moment, perplexed by Jenkins's behaviour. "By the way, what are you doing with that bottle?"

Jenkins was carefully wrapping the stoneware bottle in a sheet of waxed paper he had drawn from his pocket.

"Keeping it as a reminder, Sir," he replied. "Of your brilliance, Sir."

"Ah, very good," replied The Legend. "Because I can assure you, it has nothing to do with this case," he added, blithely ignoring the dent in the corpse's cranium.

"By the way, you don't think that asking the police to find a well-travelled Serbian dwarf with a pet snake might be a bit of a tall order, Sir? If you will excuse the pun?"

The Legend was about to answer when, to Jenkins's surprise, a short man in a wide-sleeved shirt and baggy trousers distinctly reminiscent of the style worn in Eastern Europe emerged from a house nearby. In his hand he held a small wooden cage from which a hissing sound proceeded.

"Seize him Jenkins!"

Called to act, Jenkins never let the Constabulary down. He leapt towards the Serbian with truncheon drawn, only to find that The

Legend had done exactly the same. A struggle ensued, in which Jenkins and The Legend sought to disentangle themselves from each other. In the mean time, the sawn-off Serb made his getaway, through the dark and noisome streets of Old Portsmouth.

Jenkins was still ready to fly after the fugitive, but The Legend dulled his keenness with an angry look, poking him violently in the ribs with his pipe stalk.

"It's no good Sergeant, Serbian dwarves are renowned for their fleetness of foot! By this time he'll be halfway to Timbuktu. - *And damn it, my pipe has broken!"* - he added as the stalk cracked under the repeated impact with the Sergeant's ribcage.

"Very good, Sir."

The Legend threw the pipe on the ground and glared imperiously at Jenkins.

"All that remains is for you to contact the newspapers to describe how I have solved yet another case -"

"- And how yet another villain has got away, Sir," Jenkins said with narrowed eyes, a shade of puce once again around them.

"Well, we can't get them every time." The Legend answered.

"Just once would be gratifying," Jenkins muttered under his breath as he stooped to lift something from the ground.

*

Several weeks later, in response to a knock at his door, The Legend called "Enter," in his imperious way. He was not surprised to see Sergeant Jenkins standing in the doorway, as he had done countless times before. He was holding a sheet of paper.

"Sir, I wonder if you would take a look at this."

Two large images filled with lines and whorls could be seen on the sheet.

"What is this?" The Legend asked, impatiently.

"New information, Sir," Jenkins replied. "Regarding the Case of the Left Handed Serbian Dwarf Poisoner. Not that he poisoned dwarves, you understand, Sir."

"Well, what are these?"

"Fingerprints, Sir," replied Jenkins with a flat, respectful voice. In reply to The Legend's questioning look, he explained: "Impressions left by the hands on the objects they touch, Sir. A new method of identification used to track down criminals. Have you not heard of it?"

"I have not."

"I thought not, Sir. What with you concentrating so much on the Narrative Method. Fingerprints are proving most effective in tracking down villains. Because you see, Sir, everybody's fingerprint is unique."

The Legend's eyes bulged as his Sergeant went on: "So, for example, Sir, were one to test for fingerprints something one knows a particular person has held, and compare those fingerprints with a piece of evidence an unknown felon has held, one could safely deduce that if those prints were the same, then the people who held both objects were in point of fact one and the same person, too."

"Very interesting, Jenkins, but -"

Jenkins cut him off with an impatient, raised hand.

"It appears, Sir, that the person who held the ginger beer bottle we found at the scene, which a pathologist has confirmed fits exactly into the depression in the skull of our deceased man was the same person who held the pipe you so petulantly - not wishing to be rude to you, Sir - threw on the floor at the murder scene. Do you remember, Sir? That was after poking me in the ribs with it, Sir. Quite a lot," he gazed in an offended way at The Legend for a half second. "In fact, Sir, it would seem that you and the murderous bottle-wielder share an identity," he continued as The Legend's eyes grew wide in realisation and his jaw dropped. "*Your* identity, Sir, that is," Sergeant Jenkins added, in explanation.

"Enquiries reveal that a small foreign herpetologist witnessed you smashing the poor drunken victim over the head in a fit of rage. And further enquiries reveal that the victim is none other than the cousin of the Dockyard's Paymaster and that he, neighbours inform me, claimed to have some revealing information about you and the missing strongbox in the Disappearing Donkey case."

"Jenkins, that case was closed long ago -" The Legend began, but Sergeant Jenkins raised his voice and ploughed on undeterred:

"I haven't quite finished yet, Sir. You see, in the light of his own cousin being murdered after he tried to blackmail your good self for your involvement in covering up the strongbox theft, the Paymaster has confessed that you shared the loot from that little job, Sir. There were no men with twisted lips involved. No Russians, nor donkey-lifting hot air balloons to Northern France.

"Nonsense. You saw the Serb run – a sure sign of guilt -" The Legend countered, but Sergeant Jenkins cut him off.

"True. But I found and spoke with him. In fact, he is our key witness. It turns out he ran for it when he saw you because he realised you were a police officer and that you would try, as criminal slang has it, Sir, to *fit him up*. That is why he scarpered, Sir. A sign of guilt, yes. But not his."

Sergeant Jenkins paused for a moment and drew himself to his full though inconsiderable height, as The Legend stood frozen behind his leather-covered desk.

"I am beginning to realise after years under your brilliant tuition, Sir, that murder does not usually happen because of a great narrative, as writers in Penny Dreadfuls will have us believe. No, Sir, quite the opposite. In most cases, murderer is devoid of imagination. That's why I am going to call my new approach to crime, Sir, The Gradgrind Method. In deference to you Sir, and your wonderful stories.

"Oh, and by the way, Sir. You are under arrest," added the Sergeant with a degree of satisfaction. "For murder and theft... Sir."

We buried my dad in the woods

Christine Lawrence

We buried my Dad in the woods. He didn't want a church
ceremony or to be buried in a churchyard with a slab of marble to
remember him by. He didn't want to go down the crem on that
sometimes conveyor-belt exit to the next world. He didn't really
believe in the next world. He was anti-church to the extreme - born
a Catholic, lived through the hell that was Poland in the Second
World War and never got over it - not really.

When he died, we'd not spoken for over a year - long story. Not
spoken for a year and I didn't know - my brother told me his wishes.
He wanted one of those Eco burials - to be shoved in a hole in the
woods somewhere. I was never sure whether it was his true belief
that it would be better to be recycled into the forest or just some
perverse way of sticking his fingers up at his family - a way of saying
'No-one cares about me now and I don't want you all standing
around my grave or putting flowers on a hump in some cemetery
which is connected to a church I don't believe in.'

He died in the QA and there he lay, waiting for me to work out
how the hell do you get a body from the hospital into a hole in the
woods. Not just the hole but the coffin and all that. Lucky for me
there was a leaflet on it and soon I found myself sitting in a
woodland grove, choosing the place to lay my Dad to rest. On the
side of a hill, between the trees with views of sheep on the South
Downs. I smiled and knew my Dad would love it here.

Now what about a coffin? We sat, my partner and I, in an office
bedecked with coffins - wicker, raffia, cardboard and even one of
wood. We were told we could even put my Dad in the ground
dressed just in a shroud. I thought about this for only a brief
moment before deciding on a wicker one. I shuddered at the

thought of undertakers - men in black with top hats and grim faces. But no - you don't need undertakers to bury your Dad in the woods.

The day dawned - a late November crisp and Autumn day. The kind of day I remembered the good times with my Dad by, walks in the woods near our home, kicking up the golden leaves and laughing together about life. A short drive took us to the burial site where we met with my two brothers and our children. We needed a few strong young men to help with the bier - it's a woodland walk from the Centre to the site - all downhill and bumpy. Being Autumn the ground was slippery and a little treacherous in places! My Dad was in the car - a four-wheeled drive wagon driven by the woman who ran the burial site. She'd gone to the QA that morning and with the help of the mortuary assistant had popped Dad into his new wicker coffin and there he was, lying in the back of her car. We just had to get him out and onto the wooden bier. Luckily we had strong sons to bear the weight.

My sister-in-law had made a floral decoration to place on the coffin - made of dried flowers and bound with natural fibres - no wires - and she placed this on the coffin. Then we were off.

As I said before, the ground was slippery underfoot and quite steep in places. Ever tried wheeling a bier laden with the six foot long, well-built remains of your Dad down a winding woodland path? At each twist and turn the boys struggled to control the roll of the wagon, clinging onto the coffin, giggling and joking as they went. The sun shone through the trees, now bereft of many of the golden leaves that had shimmered and danced the week before when we'd wandered this same path to find the perfect resting place.

There is something final about seeing the hole in the ground that you're about to put your Dad in. When we turned the last bend and reached the clearing where I'd sat pondering on the view it just hit me that this was it. My Dad was dead and wasn't coming back.

Now we just had to manipulate him from the bier and into the ground. Luckily the young woman who'd collected Dad from the QA was still with us - as a kind of guide. She'd talked us through the process of balancing the coffin on the boards and how to take the weight of the straps and to carefully lower him into the ground. I stood and watched. The hole was very deep and apart from the top layer of soil was completely chalk - a nightmare to dig so I imagine. Incidentally, we were given the option to dig his grave but graciously declined and were grateful for the mini-digger which was peeking from behind a tree a few yards away.

Once Dad was in his grave I felt the need to say a few words - my brothers had agreed that I should be the one - being the 'writer person' in the family. So I talked about the good things in Dad's life - and there were loads although he probably wouldn't have agreed. I talked about some of the not so good things too, just to keep a balance. Then I read a poem I'd found in a collection of John Betjeman's he'd left at his bedside - Autumn 1964. Funnily enough, reading the poem made me realise that Dad may have had some sort of belief in the afterlife and all that - the last two lines state 'And in the bells the promise tells of greater light where Love is found.'

My brother's contribution was to bring along a compilation cd that he'd bizarrely made ready for his own funeral - he was only fifty-five at the time! He insisted that he wanted to play the music as Dad was lowered into his grave. The young woman (our guide) had tried it in the Centre building before we walked to the grave and it had worked then but once at the graveside it would not work - just made a booming noise. She even ran back up to the office and came back with new batteries just to make sure - but again just this loud noise was emitted from the speaker. My brother was a little upset although I am convinced that Dad didn't really want morose music at his funeral. And it was morose. He got his own way that day.

Since then I've found talking to my Dad much easier than when he was here in person. I can say whatever I want to him now and he doesn't get upset or ignore me. We're closer now than we had been for years. And although I don't sit beside his grave very often - it's not marked other than by a crab-apple tree which was planted after the burial - every Autumn I remember our walks and he knows I love him.

Tarmo and Arayla

Jacqui Pack

In the days when the passage of time was marked by the sun, in the seasons and the festivals of The Lady, Arayla lived with her parents in a village, set half-way between the brooding hills and the river.

A delicate and fair child, pure of mind and kind of heart, Arayla grew more beautiful each year. By the time she came of age, not a boy – or man – in the village could truthfully claim they were not in love with her. But for all her admirers, only one touched her heart. Tarmo, the blacksmith's son, was a bear of a youth, with broad shoulders, dark eyes, unruly hair, and a strength that made iron bend to his will, even without the heat of the furnace.

To Arayla's delight, their families approved of the match and it was agreed that she and Tarmo would wed at the end of his apprenticeship. Following custom, the young couple exchanged tokens to bind their union. Tarmo fashioned an ornate clip to crown Arayla's golden hair, while her gift to him was a waistcoat she had spent many nights embroidering. Charged with her love and time, the woollen material became a thing of great beauty. Its front panels glimmered with silver thread, and silken birds readied themselves for flight amongst the tapestry grasses adorning its back.

Tarmo was as proud of his waistcoat as he was of wooing Arayla, and believed both to be rightfully his.

One summer's day a group of travellers arrived at the village boundary. They were performers by trade, but the village-women called them gypsy enchanters and spoke of their presence in uneasy whispers. The children, however, welcomed them without question, for their leader was a renowned storyteller and puppeteer who could conjure thrills and laughter alike.

By day, under the watchful eyes of the village-women, Pollo and his troupe entertained the young, filling their minds with excitement and music. By night, certain of the village men would walk in the shadows, hoods pulled low over their faces, to the fires and tents of the travellers. And once there, unobserved by their women-folk, they too would find entertainment.

Summoned by the tolling bells one Sunday, Arayla made her way to the Church of The Lady, her hair fastened with Tarmo's clip. As she turned into the lane she saw Pollo, sitting under a fruit-laden apple tree close to the churchyard wall, cleaning a set of engraved wooden pipes.

The sun bathed the lane and churchyard in warmth, yet shade encircled the puppeteer. The tails of his patchwork frock-coat were spread on the ground beneath him, and his leather-clad legs sprawled over the tree's roots. His eyes shone in the dense shadow and, drawn by his presence, Arayla halted, the call of the bells forgotten.

Pollo raised the pipes to his lips. A mist of shimmering music floated into the air, mellifluous sounds of corruption that muted the calling bells. Caught in a melodic net, Arayla swayed like a reed in the river. Notes danced through her soul, searching its depths, transgressing its boundaries. She put a hand to her chest, breathing deeply as the music heightened her senses. Dilated with new-born desires and longings, her eyes unfocused; the lane, and the church, faded from her consciousness. Pollo's heady refrain guided her other hand to her cheek, then up to her hair. Her fingers tugged open the metal clip, and cast it to the ground. With her halo of golden hair fallen to her shoulders and her eyes closed, Arayla swayed in forbidden ecstasy, hands stroking her pale skin.

Pollo stood and drew closer until his shadowy aura enveloped them both. Lowering the pipes, he drew an apple from his coat and raised it to his mouth. The music continued, unearthly chords weaving a hazy gauze of beguilement across the lane. Without taking his eyes from Arayla's face, Pollo bit into the apple, revealing its soft flesh, then held it to her lips. Arayla sighed. She licked a glistening smear of juice from the dip of her cupid's bow, then tilted her head, opening her mouth to receive his offering. He smiled, and teased her trembling lips with the fruit before finally holding it still.

As Arayla's teeth touched its skin, the church bells pealed out a renewed call to worship. Pollo stiffened. His music faltered, its harmonies suddenly dissonant against the chimes.

Arayla recoiled as Pollo's music fragmented, her mind and body burning with shocked awareness. Unable to break free from his gaze, she crouched and fumbled in the dirt for her clip. As the last echoing notes decayed, she grasped the metal pin, and stumbled towards the sanctuary of the church.

Pollo threw the apple to the ground, a fell expression clouding his eyes. The sun pierced the dark veil around him and he returned, alone, to the travellers' encampment.

That night, long after her parents had fallen asleep, Arayla loitered at her bedroom window, teased by the memory of Pollo's music. As the wind danced purple clouds over the moon, a flash of colour below caught her eye. She stared into the darkness of the street and after a few moments spied Tarmo, the wind blowing his cloak to reveal his beautiful waistcoat. Sleepless and curious, she watched him pass, then donned her own cloak and followed, unable to conceive of where her betrothed might be headed.

She trailed him to the bridge beyond the crossroads, where he met the other young men of the village. Together the group walked towards the forest, their talk loud and rowdy. Arayla waited until they had disappeared into the trees, then crossed the bridge, keeping her distance for fear of being spotted. Eventually, the men came to the travellers' tents and settled themselves by the camp's open fire. Creeping as close as she dared, Arayla knelt behind a scarlet rowan, wrapped her cloak around herself and watched.

The aroma of roasting meat filled the air as the travellers sang and played their instruments. To the accompaniment of guitars, pipes and drums the traveller-women brought mead to the village-men and sat amongst them, laughing and drinking. The dancing firelight cast a warm glow, and Arayla soon felt her eyelids become heavy.

Without warning the music stopped, and Pollo somersaulted into the clearing in front of the crowd. Arayla, still haunted by the sensations aroused by his music, flushed at the sight of his lithe body and wide smile. Amid welcoming cheers and applause, Pollo pulled back the canvas opening of a nearby tent and, with a flourish, cried, 'Gentlemen! Gentlemen. For your delight – Selenka!'

The crowd fell silent. A woman stepped from the tent, as if drawn out by his gesture. A magnificent woman. She stood barefoot, full coloured skirts hitched up by her be-ringed hands, nails painted and arms adorned with bracelets that wound around her skin like snakes. Her shoulders were bare, save for a glossy cascade of dark ringlets. Gold bands encircled her neck and, beneath her locks, hooped earrings gleamed. Her face, strong and proud, was unlike that of any of the village-women with its dark eyes and coloured lips.

The musicians struck up a beat and Selenka moved forwards. The music was slow at first, but Tarmo and his drunken friends clapped, shouted and cheered, and in response the dance became faster. Selenka's gold glowed in the firelight; her skirts tumbled around her thighs creating a blur of continuous colour, movement and rhythm. She span and jumped, her head high, confident, arrogant, powerful, intoxicating. Untouchable. The music grew frenzied; the dance followed. Selenka panted, stamped and gyrated, leaping as the flames did, her skin glowing in the flickering light. Fever burning in her eyes, she moved as though the music controlled her, as though it denied her peace.

Concealed behind the tree, Arayla felt dizzy. Rapt in the dance, her body remained motionless but her mind whirled and twisted along with Selenka. She felt herself floating, felt the fire's heat, the pounding of the music, the dark magic of the night all around her. She felt herself enter the dance, become the dance, and sensed others around her, a legion of souls thrashing and heaving. All held by the music. All caught within Selenka's movements. Their power inflamed her senses. With her heart beating to the passion and lust of the rhythm, Arayla abandoned herself to Selenka, her dance, and the night.

Silence, unexpected and dense, lifted Arayla out of the dance and returned her to consciousness. She found herself slumped against the rowan, her face pressed into its hard bark. The sun was climbing through the trees and birdsong filled the forest.

Confused, she stared at the clearing. The travellers, their tents and fire, had gone. The village-men were nowhere to be seen. Only a burnt patch of earth remained.

Life carried on as it had before the advent of the travellers, but from that day Arayla's heart was filled with sorrow. It seemed Tarmo had left the village, telling no one of his plans. As news of his departure spread, fresh suitors came forward but, despite her parents' pleas, Arayla shunned their wooing, refusing to believe her betrothal broken.

As the weeks became months, the sunlight left her hair and twilight fell across her eyes. Every morning she pinned her braids with Tarmo's clip and awaited his return, and every evening a little more of her delicate beauty crumbled and withered in sadness.

Twelve full circles of seasons passed. Arayla spent her mornings teaching in the schoolroom and her afternoons alone, wandering the woods, pastures and waterways that encompassed the village. On one such summer afternoon the hazy sun drove her to the river by the forest. Leaving the path, she climbed down to the cool shade under the bridge. With her feet dabbling, she lay on the bank, closed her eyes and lost herself in the pink landscape of childish daydreams.

Hoof beats and grinding steel-rimmed wheels roused her. Barefoot, she clambered up the river bank and, shading her eyes against the now lowering sun, made out a small caravan of painted wagons. Remaining hidden, she watched their approach, sensing intuitively that Pollo would be at their head.

Arayla's heart, empty for so long, filled with emotion. It pulsed to the beat of the horses' hooves, squeezed the air from her lungs, and pressed on her ribs until she thought they might snap. As the wagons rolled forward, a rush of desire seized her. She would run onto the road; be reunited with Tarmo; join with the travellers. But with the desire came shame, awakening the memory of her impious encounter in the lane. She held her breath and closed her eyes, fighting to contain the tumbling assault of impulses within. On the path, loose stones crumbled beneath the cart's weight and the troupe drove on, unaware of her struggle.

As Pollo's wagon moved by, Arayla's senses returned and she looked again at the passing caravan. Sitting on the back steps of the third wagon was a woman dressed in crimson, her head nodding with the rhythm of its motion. Selenka's undiminished dark beauty was impossible to mistake, but her vibrancy and passion had vanished. Only an empty, doll-like husk remained, gazing vacantly into the trees.

The next cart had rails running along its sides from which wooden puppets dangled in a macabre procession. Held by imperceptible strings, their lifeless limbs danced loosely at their sides and their heads lolled. A flare of sunlight amongst the marionettes drew Arayla's attention. Her heart recognised its source before her eyes had searched it out. At the end of the rail hung Tarmo, shrunken to the size of a child, his embroidered waistcoat glinting in the sun.

Fear's cold fingers stretched themselves around Arayla's soul. Reciting prayers she had learned but not valued until that moment, she crossed herself, calling upon The Lady to protect her from an evil she could not comprehend.

And, perhaps, The Lady answered her call.

While Arayla reeled under the sorrow and regret of Tarmo's sightless stare, the clip holding her braids sprung open and tumbled down the bank. It skittered over the stones and pebbles, then skimmed onto the river, bouncing twice before slipping under its surface. Distraught, Arayla hurried down the bank and plunged her hands into the water, only to see the ornate metalwork re-appear close to the river's centre, swept along by the current.

Above, on the road, the travellers' caravan entered the bridge. As the broken clip travelled under its stone arch, Pollo reined in his horse and stopped, tilting his head to one side as though listening. After a moment's concentration, he urged the beast onwards to the crossroads, the other wagons close behind.

Arayla, half-blinded by silent tears, watched Tarmo's gift dip and bob down the river, until it disappeared from view.

By the time she returned to the road, the colourful wagons were no more than dark smudges, dotted along the path which climbed south to the hills, and away from the village.

From a cobwebbed drawer

William Sutton

I can't believe Niall is dead. He was not just the first friend I'd made since moving to Portsmouth, but my first ever writing confidant. We met in the queue at an open mic night on the Eastern Road. He was reading flash fiction; I was singing my ukulele epic.

He overheard me putting my name on the list. "William George Q? Nom de plume, I presume?" That peculiar gravel in his voice; that poetic lilt. "I'm Niall. I'm new here. Beer?"

We agreed at once that performance poets were a scourge and should be ritually slaughtered. We derided novelists who leap to premature fame with their first book. Young film directors were worse. Not if it were us; that would be different.

It was a meeting of minds such as I'd never known. I never dreamt it was possible to share the pains of the creative life, and the joys. The second week, we didn't even go in for the open mic. We bought each other drinks. We talked. We talked all night. At last orders, we loaded up the table – two pints, two drams – and they had to manhandle us out at closing time. We talked and talked, and we've never stopped. Until the day of the phone call.

Electrical storms crackled over the Solent. I was racing home as the clouds broke behind me. I'd reached the sanctuary of my desk, bedraggled and freaked, when the phone rang.

Niall's number. Strange. We never interfered with each other's writing time: always write for yourself before you talk to me; always edit yourself before you edit me. Mantras we formulated down the Temperance Folk Cellars, Stamshaw Strummers, and the Unlaced Brigadier. We no longer bothered performing in the open mics; we went just to cheer ourselves up.

"What the hell do you want?" I said.

It was his wife. Niall was missing.

We began exchanging stories before we'd known each other a month: my shabby typescripts for his handwritten scrawls.

"The pen! The pen can only write, man." Niall loved declarations and manifestos. "The computer is a distraction engine. Give me pages. Fingers. Ink." His fountain pen flourishes won me over. The poetry of annotated envelopes, dark with scribbles, outshone my polished but pointless digitalia. "I need to see my mistakes. Get to know my manuscript. Crossings outs, blots of frustration. Manual labour, man."

Niall's devotion was visceral. I stashed my laptop under my desk. I returned to the tools of my youth: watermarked foolscap, ink-blotted fingers, and my old Eaton typewriter.

The fourth time we met, I got to the pub early. A woman fluttered her lashes at me. "May I sit with you?"

"Oh," I stammered. "I'm—I'm expecting a friend."

She moved on, rolling her eyes, before the barman could chase her away.

When I told him, Niall immediately wove this encounter into a story. "I met the Fallen Lady of Portsea in a threadbare den of drunkards." Corny melodrama, maybe, but it wove itself into my first novel, Four Floors of Portsea Whores. Niall turned everything into stories.

Towards the end of the night, in the whisky stages, I told him about my life, and doomed loves: the psychologist psychopath, the depressive contortionist, the divorcee mum of three who spent with glee and liked to pee.

Niall slapped his knee. "Oh, man. Why screw around with fiction? Write your life, man." He glorified my wild days: things I knew had been destructive, he idealised as obsessive and free. Niall never realised that I envied him, with his house and family.

"But I have written about my life." I hung my head. "I've tried. There's this manuscript, lurking in my desk drawer. Memoirs of my travels. Tales of lust and narcissism. I poured my heart into it, but..." I fought to hold my voice steady. These tales still hurt; and while you're hurt, you're not ready to write. "Worthless, I promise you."

"Take them out of the drawer."

I clutched the penultimate dram. "I can't."

"Need too much work, you coward?"

"Need shredding." I took a melodramatic gulp. "And the drawer's full of cobwebs."

"Scared of spiders now, man?"

"Not any old spider. It's the King of Spiders."

Niall raised his glass. "To Solomon, King of Spiders. Wisest arachnid of 'em all."

"Poor bastard." I clinked glasses. "Stuck with my stinking stories."

"He'd give good feedback."

I smote my forehead in shame. "I'd give anything if only he'd edit them."

"You kill me." Niall fell about laughing. He punched my shoulder as the barman dragged us outside. "Bring the cobwebbed memoirs. Bring 'em."

I fell asleep on the bus, staggered home, sat at my desk. I hadn't the courage to look in the drawer. But I felt released. I never brought Niall the memoirs, not the originals. I started writing afresh. New takes on those hoary anecdotes, thumped out on the Eaton in the early hours. Niall's cajoling brought me back to life.

We developed our method straightaway. Over the first Guinness, we read each other's work, relaxed and unhurried. During the second, we made notes. Thus, lightly-oiled, we launched into critique mode. No holds barred. Appreciative. Unwarranted criticism can hurt. But a sympathetic reader, and fearless, makes for creative wrangling. Cut away the dead parts. The story roars into life. Reframe the narrative. Spark that irony you get in the best books. Foreground a sentence you'd barely noticed that captures the spirit of your story. Slash those overworked paragraphs. And it fizzes into life.

Then the phone call.

It wasn't our day to meet. We never phoned each other. It was part of our old school alliance. We arranged the next meeting when we said our farewells.

I loved sharing my progress with Niall. My abilities, long

obscured by doubt and depression, were bearing fruit. (That's exactly the kind of putrid metaphor Niall would slash. Try again.) I was elated. That's all.

Am I tingeing the past rose? I still doubted my abilities. When I perused the competition listings in Writers' Magazine, I still felt my writing wasn't up to it. I hammered out that draft of Portsea Whores, it's true. But most of my typescripts I thrust into the dreaded drawer, on top of the older stories. In our drunken dialogues, I talked Niall through these inchoate ramblings, and he critiqued them, brilliantly. Every block he dissolved. Niall could always see a way forward. Over every abyss, he spied out dramaturgical bridges. Yet did I go back to improve the things? Did I bollocks. They sat in the drawer, imperfect, unrevised. I sent off the odd story. But mostly I squeezed them into the drawer of discarded dreams, like a tramp lining his clothes with newspaper to keep out the winter frost.

Niall was worse. He was the one hiding his light. His writings were deceptively simple. When I read Skid & the Dirty Underpants, over that first Guinness, I laughed, I wept. Effortless twists. Moral conundrums. And always that sense of impending doom: his forte. O why did Niall discuss my stories more than his own? I took it as confidence: he didn't need my critiques, or my approbation.

Maybe the opposite was true: Niall was an incisive editor, but didn't rate his own ideas; maybe he thought I didn't rate them. I don't know.

We didn't talk about that. We didn't talk about family, news, politics, or music. We only talked writing. How to shape stories. Who were good writers, who was overrated. What made a good sentence, what was bad. What purpose have semi-colons; what are commas for. How come we were the only ones who valued these things when nobody else seemed to care. And the next week, and the next.

Until Niall's wife, Daisy, rang.

I was just back at my desk, bedraggled from the storms. The ringing filled me with eerie premonitions.

"Niall's missing," said Daisy.

I couldn't speak.

Missing? Jesus, Niall would never go missing. He stayed home all day writing; he went for a run on Tuesdays, drank with me on Thursdays; the rest of the week, he stayed home. How could he go missing? He took the kids to school, while Daisy worked; he fetched them home. Some writers might vanish on retreats to deepest Devon, or forget to mention their Hysterical Harrogate History conference, or go on lost weekends. Not Niall. Niall was not the sort to go missing.

"He went for his run," said Daisy, "like he does. Only he hasn't come back. And these electrical storms... I'm afraid."

I was not sufficiently sympathetic. The deadline for the Portage Prize was looming. I'd made progress with the sequel to Portsea Whores, and I needed Niall to sort out my characterisation. Hanging Haiti's Heart-throb was all in place: the motivations were credible, the dialogue was sharp, but it was too close to ordinary life. These characters ought to lacerate each other; I'd written a series of genial altercations. Niall would blast away the soporific carapace. Catastrophe was his forte. He'd look it over.

"I see what's wrong," he'd say, and not only that: "I can fix it."

In the early weeks, I fought my corner. I'd grudgingly agree, while explaining my intentions.

As I worked through Niall's rewrites, I'd discover the bastard was right. Intentions be damned: I'd got it wrong; he'd told me how to fix it. What else mattered?

These days I could anticipate what Niall would say. In fact, I'd begun to take his advice before he even gave it. I remember his face when he finished Portsea Whores, that engaging smile of his. "I have taught you everything I know, man."

What would he say of Haiti's Heart-throb? It's realistic, it's nice; but relationships in stories have a price. Trash them. Hurt the ones you love. I was ready to rewrite. But I needed his input. These bloody deadlines – TDC Award, Momentary Fictions – what was he doing going missing?

Daisy was full of theories. He'd hit his head. Had a fit. An absence. A fugue state.

It sounded more like a story than real life to me. He might be in hospital somewhere; the bastard never carried his blasted phone, let alone ID.

She'd rung the hospital. Now she would call the police.

"The police?" I said. "Call the literary police. I need him back."

It was Thursday, our day to meet, and still no news. I didn't call Daisy. I just went along, as normal. I don't know why. I wasn't denying that he was gone. I half-expected the sly old bastard to turn up, with some tall tale. I bought myself drinks all night, right down to the two pints and two drams. When I got home, I went to my desk. It's always a stupid idea to write drunk. But it gave me courage.

I opened the drawer. The dreaded drawer. The cobwebbed drawer of malevolent dreams. Niall told me to do it, all those weeks ago. But that was before he taught me how to edit. For years, rewriting was such a tribulation that I avoided it with the zeal of the true phobic. Befriending Niall changed all that. Rewriting became a glorious opportunity. My raw material was good; now I was ready to take the world by storm.

I pulled out my memoir, that pile of drivel I had so long tried to forget. I stared at it, bewildered.

There were scrawls all over the typescript. Handwriting. Spidery handwriting.

Handwriting not my own. Scribbling our edits in the pub, we developed a code, I suppose, a shorthand, like teenage girls who copy their best friend's mannerisms. These notes, though, I definitely hadn't made. At least, I had no memory of making them. I could have done it, drunk. It looked more like Niall's scrawling. When had he seen this typescript? I never showed it to him. I hadn't taken anything from this drawer, not for years; I'd only stuffed in more irretrievable tales. This was the pessimism Niall pooh-poohed; and that's what persuaded me to write again. Cut the bluster, strengthen the through-line, tell the tale lean and fresh.

"Everything can be rewritten," Niall said. That was one of his favourites. It's like he broke into my house and did it himself to prove it to me.

Stupid, drunken thoughts. I shook them off.

I found myself staring at the notes. I couldn't help it. You see your typescript annotated, and you have to look, even if you fear the worst. Christ, they were good, these notes. When the reader gets it, really gets it, it's painful, but it's precious. Such an editor wields the chisel and unshackles the life from the lumpen stone. Out it soars: a new creation.

I was so wound up about Niall, I stayed up. I made the changes, I typed it up anew. That Niall was missing was awful; to edit was easy. I finally dozed off, there at my desk, after typing the new title page: The Halter of Gibraltar.

When I awoke, sun was pouring through the skylight, illuminating the typescript, neatly stacked, on which I had dribbled.

I regarded it with awe and dread. I couldn't look now; I would check it later. I reached for the drawer, the cobwebbed drawer. As I opened it, a great hairy-arsed spider scuttered out at me.

I flung the story at him. The bastard terrified me. I only meant to shove it back in the drawer. I never meant to harm. I always rescue spiders; kill them, and it rains for forty days.

I peered into the drawer. There he lay, spasming, on his back; I'd crushed his legs.

I was appalled. I never meant anything by it. He lay there, unable to move. I did my best to rescue him. I scooped him on to the title page, fighting my revulsion, and tilted him out the skylight. He might survive.

He slid down to the roof. His future didn't look bright; but he might survive. It began raining.

After that, I'm not sure what order things happened in. That whole day is hazy. At some point, I packaged up the rewrite to send to the Portage Prize. That felt good. I fell asleep, shattered. Daisy called. I'd promised to check in with her, and I hadn't.

"They've found Niall."

"Thank God. I thought you were going to tell me something awful."

She paused, her breath hollow down the phone. "Like what?"

"I don't know." I faltered. "Like, he's fallen. Broken something."

"I don't know what he broke. But he's dead."

I jumped to my feet so fast, I hit my head on the skylight. The world went out of kilter. I searched for something to say, something sensitive, or meaningful. My jaw worked pointlessly up and down. My addled wits weren't up to it. On the roof outside, a magpie was tugging at the run-off pipe.

"Come over." Daisy's voice was small and broken. "Would you?"

The way Niall died, it never made sense to me. One minute, your heart's beating; the next minute, it's not. Bruising on his legs. Cause of death never identified.

Don't ask me to explain. I can't. I couldn't even speak at the funeral. The night before, I was writing my speech. Homily, eulogy, whatever. It was the first time I'd gone back to my desk since the news. I don't know what I was looking for. I opened the drawer. Underneath the Gibraltar memoir, I found the next bit of my typescript, an incident from my travels I'd written up as a play years ago. I hadn't noticed when I looked that other night, drunk, but it bore the same scrawls. Could it be my handwriting after all? The story was okay, as I remembered it: moving, funny, a contrived ending. Until the scrawl. I looked through the edits. Yes, yes, yes. Each suggestion was spot on: heightened tension; bolder characterisation; cheap jokes sharpened into emotional cliffhangers.

I never wrote the eulogy. I made a weak excuse, and left it to his wife.

Daisy thanked me for my support. She grabbed me after the service. "I want you to have these." She handed me a brown manila envelope. "I can't bear to look at them."

No more could I. Niall's own stories, unpublished, unknown. I stashed them – where else? – in the cobwebbed drawer. I was ashamed. When I should have been writing Niall's eulogy, I wrote up the changes to my old manuscript instead. I couldn't help it: the notes were so perfect, so easy to put into practice, and neatly turned into a local thriller: Death in a Dakar Dockyard. First came production at the New Theatre Royal; then the Tindall prize, and West End transfer. It's not Shakespeare, but Dockyard still runs in schools and provincial theatres.

It was just the same with all my half-baked manuscripts. Next in the drawer came Mutilated in Mumbai, and A Seattle Shooting, then The Great Gdansk Garrotting – but you've heard of these. They were easy to adapt for radio. It seemed inevitable the way the TV and film followed.

Daisy moved in. Things happen, you can imagine, in grief. She was adamant I shouldn't change my writing setup, not now the successes were flowing. Niall would have wanted that more than anything. My house was closer to the kids' school. Easier for them to move. Besides, it would have been too uncanny to move into Niall's:

to sit at his desk, to sleep in his bed.

By the time of my commission from the National Theatre, I was all out of ideas. I scratched around for a while, hedging with my agent and the NT's director. I was making progress, I told them.

Lies.

I couldn't give up. I had responsibilities to Daisy and the kids; to Niall. I knew what I had to do. It was a while since I'd risked opening the cobwebbed drawer. In the flush of success, I'd all but emptied it: the tales I'd told Niall, those memoirs so beautifully annotated in the drawer, were used up. What was left? I peered in, quaking, fearful of the spider, though I knew he was long gone.

One thing lay forgotten among the cobwebs, or ignored: the manila envelope.

A siren sounded down the road.

Niall's stories. I slid them out, sheepishly. That spidery scrawl, definitely his, however similar our annotations looked. That children's book he was working on. The edits were meticulously written in. I simply had to type it up.

I had a pang, as I typed my name on the cover sheet. But what difference? The money would come to Daisy and the kids as surely as if I admitted it was his. Besides, it was as much my work as his, we'd analysed the story in such detail. I stacked it neatly, blue flashing lights illuminating the pages for a moment, and typed an envelope addressed to the National Theatre; they lapped up these old-fashioned habits of mine. Everything can be rewritten, Niall would say. I changed a couple of characters' names, as you do, to put my stamp on it. Typing it up even felt like I really was typing one of my own stories, but edited to Niall's exacting standards: each character with an intricate backstory, every conflict a turning point, each crisis nuanced.

The manila envelope wasn't empty. I knew he'd finished one book, but not the whole series: Skid Steals His BFF's GF, Skid & the Typewriter Threads. I wouldn't look now. I'd get to the postbox. Gingerly reopening the cobwebbed drawer, just a peep, I was sliding the manila envelope back in when they ran at me: Mrs Spider, and her little ones. I don't know what possessed me. Old Solomon Spider's brood didn't stand a chance. Before I knew what I was doing, I was scraping them off the desk, my heart pounding. I tossed their remains out the skylight. Daisy would laugh when I told her. I'd explained, sort of, about the original spider; how I'd found the annotations, and the shock he'd given me. She'd laughed. My stories cheered her up. I never said I'd killed him. She was so down, after Niall; I did what I could to lighten her mood.

Daisy used to wish we'd gone to look for Niall. We wouldn't have saved him; he was dead before he hit the ground; but she felt guilty, carrying on without him. Thriving without him. Everything can be rewritten. She had these absences. All blank and moon-eyed. I used to worry about her driving. Picking up the kids. Crossing the road by the schoolgates, with the cars whizzing to and fro.

The traffic outside was dying down: the end of the school day. They'd be home any minute. I'd been longer typing than I realised. They should have been home long since. The blue lights were flashing right outside. There was a knock at the door.

Talk to me

Sue Shipp

Leaning heavily on her walking stick, Ethel stopped, grimacing at the ache in her knees. *Arthritis*, old Doc Farrell had said, his face creasing with that tight- lipped smile that made her want to smack him. The walk into town wasn't far, not for young knees, but Ethel's knees had been on the go for nearly eighty years and on this damp day they had been reluctant to do anything at all, let alone climb back up from the town. But it was Thursday, and Thursday was sausage day. Frank liked his sausages on Thursday. Fat, pink pork sausages in shiny skins. She'd do them right today, roll them round the pan so they would be evenly browned, just like Frank liked.

As she was walking by the shell of St Dunstan's, an abandoned church propped with scaffolding and pinned with keep out signs, a mangy dog scurried before her, teats swollen with milk. It made its way up the street, head down, sniffing at the bins. It turned, loping toward her, a dull pink tongue lolling from its mouth. Raising her stick, Ethel jabbed at it. With a swiftness that surprised her, the dog darted by. She felt the roughness of its fur on her leg as she tumbled to her knees, her bag flying from her grasp. The sausages, wrapped in white paper, rolled in a lazy arc toward the gutter, the packet spilling open.

With a yelp the dog snatched the sausages and ran toward St Dunstan's. Darting between the scaffolding poles, the sausages trailing from its mouth.

*

'But Ethel, you just bought sausages.' Big Brenda hitched up her jeggings wishing she hadn't had Harry's 'Big Breakfast'.

'Yes, I know. But the dog got them, and now I have to have some more. They're for Frank's tea.'

Brenda leaned over the counter. 'And your knee's bleeding.'

'It's only a graze. Now, you going to serve me, or what?' Ethel blew out a sigh. She'd known Brenda long enough to know she'd been a floozy, that's how she ended up with the twins, no money and no man. But floozy or no, she had tried to do right by her boys. One of them had even gone to the Grammar School; there wasn't much to be said for the other one. Too much like his father.

Brenda slapped a string of fat, shiny pink sausages on the scales. 'Did you say they're for your Frank?'

'I did. And don't be looking at me like that. I've not lost my marbles. I've been to see that Medium, you know, her who comes to the Spiritual Church on Wednesdays. She's been trying to talk to Frank, but typical of him, he has to be cussed. She says he's there; he just won't come through. She said it might be an idea to do something he would have liked, and he liked his sausages on a Thursday evening. So, if you don't mind.' Ethel opened her purse. She hadn't meant to tell Brenda anything. It surprised her how easily the words had come out.

'Put your money away.' Brenda pulled her apron over the mass of short red spikes that passed for a hairstyle. 'Come on, I'll walk with you, make sure you get home this time.'

'I'm not senile, and I do know my way home.' Ethel sniffed trying to ignore the throbbing in her knee. Taking a tumble hadn't done much for her arthritis and neither had the second walk to the Market Hall, but it was the only place in town where the butcher still served meat wrapped in bright white paper: just how Frank used to buy them.

As much as Ethel disliked Big Brenda's pushy attitude, she had to acknowledge the Market Hall had only reopened after a robust campaign by Brenda, who had badgered the local councillor; she'd made a nuisance of herself at the council offices, and had spent a night in the cells after becoming a public nuisance in the High Street. Charged with causing an affray, she had been fined eighty pounds plus costs and banned from entering the new shopping arcade for two weeks. But that had not stopped Brenda; she had canvassed, cajoled and threatened until the Market Hall was reopened.

Some said she knew things about the local councillor that his wife wouldn't have liked to hear. Ethel thought folks just liked to make a nonsense out of nothing. But for all Brenda's efforts, Ethel didn't think it was anything like as good as the original Market Hall, when her and Frank, on a brisk winter's day would stand just inside the doors eating steaming hot black pudding covered in vinegar, or buy bags of broken biscuits when he was on flat money.

*

'Give me your key, Ethel, and I'll pop the kettle on.'

Big Brenda tugged at the waistband of her jeggings, the stiletto heel of her boot finding the crack in the paved back street. There were more cracks than paving slabs these days. Nothing grew amongst these cracks, not unless you counted the cigarette butts.

Ethel handed it over, really wishing Brenda would leave her be. It wasn't just the tumble that had shaken her; it was the dog.

It was so like the one that her son, David, had brought home all those years ago. Right down to the colour of its mangy coat. It had followed David home from school that day when the snow had been building. They'd both left footprints in the yard, and on the kitchen floor.

David had insisted the dog sleep on his bed, and for a while it had stayed, dirtying the floors with it paws and growling at her whenever she spoke sharply to David. But when she had gone to slap David for his cheek, the dog had gripped her skirt in its jaws. It hadn't hurt her, and she hadn't slapped David, but she decided there and then the dog had to go.

She had waited until Frank had gone to work and David to school, and then took it to the pound, in the next town. She told them both the dog had run away. It had been days before David stopped trawling the area calling for it – and that had been at her insistence.

Thinking back, she could see that was then he started spending more time with Frank. But even so, it came as a shock when he left.

David had lied to her, to both of them, telling them he was going away for a few days with a friend. She hadn't been happy about it and when Frank had told her to let the boy go and enjoy himself, she had carried on until David had left in the slamming of the door. In the early days he had sent a few letters to Frank, and the odd birthday card, but by the time Frank died there hadn't been contact for years.

Things weren't the same after David left. She knew Frank blamed her for the rift even though he never voiced his thoughts, and she had thought it best to let things be. She had let things be after Frank died, too.

But of late, on those dark, damp nights when the burn in her knees had bitten deep, she sat on the edge of the bed weeping at the sadness of it all, thinking perhaps she should write. That thought dissolved in the morning light, for if she was being truthful, she didn't think David deserved to know, and she didn't think he would care.

But she cared. She cared a lot.

*

Frank's death was a shock.

He'd been to see old Doc Farrell for a once-over. 'It's wear and tear on the knees, Frank, and just a small problem with scarring on your lungs, but nothing that'll see you off anytime soon,' Farrell had said.

A week later Frank was dead.

She'd found him slumped on the living room floor, like some oversized rag doll, and although she had run next door to use their telephone, she knew he was gone.

In the early days, it was as if Frank was still in the house. She could smell him on his overcoat, and there was a shallow indent on his side of the bed, and they still talked. Each night she would tell him about her day, her whispered voice breaking the silence in the bedroom, and he would mostly find his way into her dreams. Sometimes he was just a fragment in the dream, other times the whole of him would be there, and she would feel young and happy. But then, Frank stopped coming, and it seemed no amount of whispering in the dark helped.

*

'Ethel? You okay, Ethel?' Brenda patted Ethel on the hand. She'd finished her tea and was getting ready to go.

'Yes. I was just thinking about Frank.' Ethel forced a smile. 'It seems he doesn't want to talk to me.'

'Ethel,' Brenda spoke softly, 'this Medium you're seeing. What else has she said?'

'Oh, that Frank may be more inclined to come through if we held the session here. She, Denise, that's her name, said she should hold something Frank valued. That'll have to be his watch, the one they gave him on his retirement. She's coming just after lunch, about one-ish.'

'I'll be round just before, Ethel. I'll bring some cakes, and you can get the kettle on.'

*

The rain had been driving hard all morning, slashing through the grey town as if trying to wash away the grime. Denise arrived just as Brenda put her finger to the doorbell. They were both glad to sink into the warmth of Ethel's tiny living room, the fire stoked to an orange roar.

Seated at a table covered in fine linen and laid with best china, they eyed each other over the cream cakes.

Ethel broke the silence. 'I'm sorry, Denise, I should have rung to tell you that Brenda was interested in coming. I hope you don't mind.' She placed Frank's watch on the table. 'I think this might help us today.'

'Brenda, I sense, you do not believe.' Denise pushed her plate to one side, taking Frank's watch in her hands. She offered a dreamy smile. 'It is a pity. You lose so much by closing your mind, and it may make it difficult for Frank to connect with us.' Denise paused for a moment. 'So I would ask you, for Ethel's sake, to quell your doubt and keep your mind open to whatever may happen. To anything I say, Ethel will only answer, yes, no, or maybe. You should know that it is possible for more than one spirit to come through at a time. Often they come with messages for loved ones, but if Ethel does not know them, I will thank them for coming and ask them to step aside.

Please remember, I am only the conduit. I cannot summon a spirit. This is not an exact science.'

Brenda bit down on the words foaming in her mouth. Hard words, with a knife's edge. She pursed her lips as Ethel broke into a girlish smile, the excitement in her eyes almost palatable.

'Ethel, have you invited Frank in today?' Denise held the watch to the side of her face.

She nodded, not trusting herself to speak, fiddling with her wedding ring, turning it round and round. It used to sit tight but the only thing stopping it from falling off these days was the swollen knuckle.

Denise closed her eyes. She breathed slowly and rhythmically, allowing her head to roll forward.

Brenda wanted to laugh. It was all so dramatic. But she could see how Ethel had been persuaded, and it disgusted her to think that a lonely old woman was being taken advantage of this way. She looked at the clock. Another five minutes and she would break up this charade.

Denise lifted her head. She opened her eyes, staring at a place just behind Ethel's head. 'Frank is close today. I can feel him. He feels calm...happy. He says it's not his turn. He's pushing someone forward...hyacinths, I can smell hyacinths.' Denise shook her head. She frowned. 'Maurice. Do you know a Maurice?'

Ethel frowned. 'No.'

'His hands are calloused. He has a wide smile. He's wearing pyjamas, but says he's better now. He says you mustn't worry. You're safe.'

Brenda felt a prickle of unease settle at the back of her neck. She moved her head from side-to-side, trying to loosen the tension in her shoulders. The warmth in the room felt stifling. The sweetness of the cream slice cleft itself to the dryness of her mouth.

'Maurice says thank you.' Denise spoke softly. 'His energy is weakening...I'm sorry...they've gone.'

Ethel slumped back in her chair, a slight frown passing across her face. 'It's just like my Frank to wait his turn. He couldn't stand queue jumping. Your dad was called Maurice, wasn't he, Brenda?'

Struggling to breathe, Brenda stood, scrabbling in her bag for her inhaler. 'I have to go, Ethel. I don't feel right...I'll see you later.'

*

The driving rain greyed around her, holding Brenda close to thoughts that with each passing year she had buried deeper and deeper, until she could almost convince herself it had never happened. But it had. And now those thoughts scrambled over each other, tearing their way out of her memory.

It happened on a bright spring morning, on his sixtieth birthday. The bedroom had been warm. Too warm. The scent from the small bowl of blue hyacinths on the table under the window fused with the sour cheese smell of sickness, making her feel light-headed.

Maurice had lain staring out of the window, or maybe he had been looking at the hyacinths. She couldn't tell. He said they reminded him of when he was a lad at school, when the wooden tubs that flanked either side of the entrance had been full of them. She had never thought of him as a lad, he was just Dad.

Throughout the night she had paced the house listening to him moan in pain. By the time the shafts of spring sunlight filtered through the windows, she had decided.

It had been simple in the end. In silence she had offered a cocktail of pills, as many as she thought he could swallow. And in silence he had taken them. She worried they wouldn't be enough, that he would be left whole but damaged. She sat holding his hand, until his grip softened, with not a word spoken between them.

It was by St. Dunstan's that Brenda stopped, her body curving into a lean. From within the shadows, the mangy dog watched, its dull pink tongue lolling from its mouth. It scented an emotion in the woman, a feeling that had been held inside her for years, eating at her. It was not a good smell, and not one that could easily be washed away.

Brenda gave a dry heave, and then another, and another until the vomit splattered across her boots, sliding into the torrent in the gutter. She watched it ride the water all the way to the vortex above the drain, and then it was gone.

The dog sniffed the air again. The scent of guilt had gone. Softly, the dog padded through the empty shell of the church.

The kamikaze male

Maggie Sawkins

The woman had been reading about spiders for eight days but was getting nowhere. The book lay open on the bedside cabinet next to the clock and a photograph of Motey. She read a chapter on The Suitor Phenomenon and The Kamikaze Male and fell asleep.

The next evening Motey came to stay. He bought the woman marigolds and a jar of stem ginger wrapped in tissue. She placed the marigolds in a vase on the table and sat opposite him with a bottle of Muscadet. As usual, he began to boast about his band, The Crooners, and their latest gig. His arms were bent at right angles on the edge of the table, and his head, which was round and white and almost hairless, sank into his shoulders.

'Well, that's enough about me,' he said at last reaching for her hand. 'How about you? Have you finished that book you're writing?'

'It's just a story,' she replied getting up. 'Would you like some coffee?'

'I'd prefer something else, but that'll do for now,' he said watching her sway across to the sink to fill the kettle. 'Well, have you finished your story then?'

'Not quite – but it won't be long.' The woman slowly stirred the coffee and placed it before him on the table. 'I suppose there were lots of young women there – at the gig?'

'A few. None as ravishing as you, of course. Come here.'

'In a minute,' she replied, unwrapping the blue tissue from the gift he had brought her.

Motey watched as she placed a piece of ginger in her mouth. While she was chewing, she lowered her eyelids and nonchalantly tore the blue tissue into shreds.

'Which do you prefer,' she said at last, 'the beauty of inflection, or the beauty of innuendo?'

'What's this? Not another feckin' philosophy lesson?'

'The act of sex – or just after?'

'Well, that's easy,' said Motey relieved. 'Why do you ask?'

The woman stared across at him as he finished his coffee. 'It was just a thought,' she replied.

'You're a strange one,' said Motey moving across and reaching for her waist. 'You're getting quite a little pot there,' he began, but before he could finish he stumbled back. 'That's strange,' he said, 'I feel quite queasy. I think I might have to go to call it a day.' And then he said no more.

After finishing the wine and the stem-ginger, the woman opened the door to the garden.

A white cat crawled from underneath a lavender bush. The woman scooped it up and carried it to her bed. The cat hadn't eaten for five days and its haunches could be felt through its fur. Unable to sleep, the woman took out her notebook. But nothing came.

She awoke in the night feeling nauseous. She went through her alphabet of insects: aphid, beetle, cockroach, damselfly, earwig ... in the hope that the repetition would lull her to sleep. By the time she'd reached w for weevil she was wide-awake.

She turned on the light, picked up her book and reread the section on The Ambush Strategies of the Trapdoor Spider until her eyes grew heavy. She dreamt she was flying naked with the cat through the clouds. It was light as a parcel of chicken feathers.

In the morning, the woman was woken by the sound of the dustcart in the road outside. She left the cat sleeping while she went downstairs.

Just then the door squeaked open and the cat made its way to a dish on the floor which contained slivers of chicken. After staring at it for a moment, the cat turned away. There was a slight breeze and a few yellow petals fell from the vase onto the table. The woman went over and flicked them to the floor where Motey was lying, as if asleep.

The cat crawled under the table. The woman picked it up, took it to her bed and lay down beside it. The cat's breathing had quickened and the skin around his mouth was as yellow as haddock. She drifted off. When she woke up the cat was dead.

After taking a shower, the woman caught sight of herself in the full length mirror and placed a hand over her rounding stomach. She made herself a cup of weak beef tea, took her books downstairs to the room in the basement, and sat at her desk. Beside the computer was a photograph of Motey, in black satin waistcoat, standing beside a double bass. He was smiling. The woman turned the photograph over, and read aloud from the chapter on The Suitor Phenomenon and The Kamikaze Male:

'Even the most violently hostile reception may not be enough to repel a male   driven to gamble on a final last-gasp mating before the female lays her eggs.'

At last she picked up her pen and began to write.

When she had finished, the woman went out to the garden and dug two holes. She rested for a while then went upstairs to the bedroom. The cat was on the pillow. Its head had lolled to one side and its silvery tongue poked from the corner of its mouth. She lifted it up.

In the garden the sun was shining. The woman gently laid the cat in one of the holes. In the other she put the photograph, and Motey's shoes wrapped in brown paper. She sprinkled both with marigold petals and covered them up with earth.

Emily

Jennie Rawling

Emily is waiting to die. There's no-one but the pots and pans to hear her confession. And God. But Emily stopped believing in God a long time ago.

She wanders into the living room, her mottled old sweater brushing the dresser top as she aims at the settee. Her unsteady legs meander a little off course but she rights herself, shaking her head in frustration. Her soft white curls bounce – the only thing with any bounce left. Once upon a time she was beautiful, all flowing auburn locks and bright blue eyes. But then, she supposed all women thought they were beautiful once.

Now a filmy grey mist covers her tired eyes, and the skin that once felt so toned and supple sags and hangs off her bones. She is tired, and bit by bit she is withering away. But to what? A long time ago she would have said that age was merely another part of the journey, of the adventure of life. That though her mortal body was dying, her spirit would grow stronger with each step of the way, and one day she would have earned her place with God.

She laughs sourly, a dry, grating sound, full of cynicism and resignation. If the pots and pans could flinch, they would. How foolish she had been in her younger years. How full of desperate hope, clinging on to the wasted belief that it would all be ok, that there was something better than this, something brighter. If only she had known. But then, what difference would it have made? Would it have made her behave any better, laugh any longer than she did? Would this hollow pain she's carried all these years be any lighter? She doubts it.

Thirty years ago she lost God, gave up on him. He proved to Emily that he had stopped believing in her, so that was when she stopped believing in him. It was her third pregnancy, her third little person inside her, warming her soul as he warmed her body. She'd finally managed to deal with the loss of the other two enough to try again. You never really get over losing a child, even if they never made it out into the world, but Emily had decided that what was meant to be was meant to be – it was all part of God's plan – and this time it would finally work out. She had done her suffering, and now she would be rewarded. This time her child would live.

As the days and weeks and then months passed by, a beautiful joy overtook her, and emanated from her in everything she did. A simple trip to the shops became a pleasure, as she imagined all the yummy things she would buy for little Harry once he was old enough for solids and sweet treats. A walk outside in the sunshine became a delight for the senses, as she plodded happily along, growing heavier and heavier. Her skin basked in the warm glow, her eyes smiled at the rays of light filtering down through the trees. The delicate scent of the flowers tickled her nose, and she massaged her bump with a deep contentment she had never before known.

John had built a crib for the first baby, which they'd banished to the loft in agony after the second miscarriage. Now they finally felt brave enough to bring it out, and they placed it proudly in their little bedroom, right at the foot of the bed where they would be able to hear little Harry gurgle and watch him play.

It was John who had come up with the name Harry. And Harrietta if it was a girl. They didn't know for sure, but they just felt it was a boy. Emily had wanted the sex to be a surprise, had thrilled at the not knowing, but after a few months John starting referring to her growing bump as Harry, and so it just stuck.

She was 24 weeks into the pregnancy when John decided a week out in the open air of the countryside would do her good. She'd been working too hard, he said. Her job as a receptionist at the law firm wasn't particularly demanding, but she did spend a lot of time on her feet, running messages here and there and basically sorting everyone else out, as was her nature. A few days of putting her feet up in the sunshine wouldn't hurt, so she agreed and off they went one Friday evening, the Morris Minor chugging away as they set off for the hour's drive.

Emily had been a big fan of headscarves in those days, thinking they made her look glamorous, and she wrapped a bright polka dot affair tightly around her head as they headed off with a vroom. She can remember that polka dot scarf even now, though it seems like a lifetime ago. It's funny, how little details can stick in your head when other ones fade.

She pushes herself up off the settee with some difficulty and a loud crack from somewhere in her pelvic region, then pads across the worn carpet and through into the bedroom. She doesn't know why she wants to see it, but all of a sudden it seems vitally important to her that it's there. That she can look at it one last time. A painful reminder of happier times and the moment when they crashed down into darkness. It will hurt to see it again, but it can't hurt any more than it already does.

Fumbling around in a bottom drawer she finds a flat cardboard box. The lid is frayed and soft around the edges, and slips off easily. Within, Emily can feel something cold and hard – another box maybe – and then she finds it. The soft fabric crinkles between her fingers as she pulls out the scarf, disturbing a few old coins that clatter against each other in the box.

"Look at those fields," John said, pointing at the sheets of yellow to their right. "I've never seen sunflowers so big."

Emily nestled her chin into the little dip on his left shoulder as she gazed happily at the beauty around them. Bliss like this was a rare thing, and she wanted to capture it and hold it tightly in her memory. "Do you think Harry will be this beautiful?" she asked.

John looked at her a moment before returning his eyes to the winding road. "Of course he will," he said. "He'll be the most beautiful thing in the world. And he'll be all ours." A slow smile spread across his face until it seemed to stretch out into the air around him, his joy radiating a warmth that enveloped Emily like a cosy blanket. Life couldn't get more perfect than in that beautiful moment.

The following morning she woke to see the sheets covered in blood. There had been no pain, no agony in the night. It had all happened by stealth. God had stolen him while she was sleeping. Like the others, little Harry was gone.

"He's in a better place now," John said. "He's with God." But even John didn't believe that any more. She could hear it in his voice.

It broke John as much as it did her. A cold tear rolls heavily down her cheek as she remembers his smile, his touch, the warmth of his hand as he cupped her chin in his palm. He was her best friend. There only ever was him, always him. He made it worth carrying on. It was just him and her against the world after Harry died. They never cared much for company anyway, but after they lost him they seemed to block the rest of the world out, clinging to one another as if the slightest breeze could take one of them away, leaving the other cold and alone. Then, two months ago, it finally did take John away, leaving Emily behind.

She presses the scarf to her eyes and it catches the tears sitting there. She won't let herself cry, not now, not today. She's been waiting for this moment to come. There's no point wasting tears, she's already made her mind up. She's suffered without them all for too long, and now John's gone what is there left? Slowly and carefully, she wraps the polka dot scarf around her head, and for just a moment she feels like a girl again. Like that beautiful young woman with the flowing auburn locks and the precious little life growing inside her. It gives her courage, to do what she has been waiting to do since they carried John away, his hands now cold and unkind.

She shuffles out into the hallway and turns right, coming to a stop outside the room. The door in front of her is smooth and painted blue. Blue for a boy. Harry's room. She hasn't been in since John left. Grasping the handle in her frail fingers she turns and gives a push. The door slowly opens to the little room beyond, with its patterned wallpaper and light blue curtains. In the corner sits the crib, still waiting. She runs her finger along the edge and disturbs a recent settling of dust. Until two months ago, her and John had cleaned the room every week, vacuuming the carpets and dusting the skirting board. It was Harry's room. They had to keep it nice for him.

There's a fleecy blanket folded in the crib, and Emily reaches in to get it, unfolding the fabric and wrapping it around her tightly. Carefully, she makes the painful descent to the ground and curls up into a ball on the carpet, bringing her bony knees in as far as they will allow it. She slips a hand into her trouser pocket and pulls out a dull silver locket. It once shone brightly, and was a pretty little thing when it was new. After years nestled against her chest its sheen has gone, but its contents are no less precious. She opens it with her fingernail and smiles at the two faces looking up at her. On the left is a much younger Emily, the picture taken in her twenties, not long after her and John started courting. The picture on the right shows a handsome young man, with a strong jaw and a wide grin. John was a real looker back then. She'd never met anyone so handsome.

She brings the locket to her lips and kisses his picture, then carefully closes it and works the thin chain over her head. Pressing the metal against her chest, she rests her head down and waits. They say old people sometimes die because they simply give up living. Emily doesn't know if this is possible, but she knows she is ready to go. There is nothing left for her here but pain and emptiness, and John and their children are waiting for her. She doesn't know if she will ever see them again, after all she stopped believing in heaven when she stopped believing in God, but she hopes she will. Somehow, despite the cynicism, despite the doubts, and the fear that what meets us after life is nothing but blackness, a little voice deep inside her tells her she will see them again. It tells her they are waiting; John with his warm safe hands ready to hold her tight once again, the children with their big trusting eyes and their chubby little fingers and hugs for mummy. She holds on to that thought tighter than anything she's ever wanted in her life. Then she slowly closes her tired eyes, and waits for the end.

"I'm coming Harry, Katie, Tom. Mummy's coming," she says, and she thinks she can hear them playing, not so far away.

"I'm coming John." She smiles. "We'll all be together, just like we dreamed of."

The perfect husband

Margaret Jennings

Gwen says love is a fool's game. It brings you dead children, cold winters and callouses on your hands. The sharp intake of breath as you haul icy water from the well.

Gwen came from the grave, that's what people say and that's why she's known as a witch. She tells the tale of how her mother's body was thrown into a collective grave and Gwen was expelled as a natural process of death. It was luck that made the madman hear the baby Gwen's cries. It was luckier still that the silk robe of the woman next to her mother led some to believe that she was one from a fancy house. Through the years this special blood was magnified by rumour to that of royalty. But Gwen followed her heart and watched women marry above their station while she lived and loved in a cottage with an earth floor with the boy who won her heart at sixteen and carried her love with him to the grave. His name was Jim. He was buried next to twelve of their sixteen children. Gwen watched while the children of lesser women slept in silken sheets, rode in fine carriages and survived into adulthood. She swore that her grandchildren would not make the same mistake that she had made. For much as she loved Jim, Gwen felt the loss of her children in her every waking hour.

Everyone said that Bella, Gwen's granddaughter was beautiful. They said her looks must have come from Gwen's royal blood on her father's side. Alice, Bella's mother, would look up from the floor she was scrubbing and say, "Who am I then ? The pig's arse?"

"Pig's arse?" said Gwen, "Course you're not the pig's arse but anyone can see that Bella's looks will buy her a place in the poshest of houses. That and her royal blood."

"Ain't no royal blood gonna get her nowhere round here, there ain't no rich people going spare."

Now Gwen had a sharp mind that gathered information like the ground gathers the grain when winnowing. She knew the names of neighbours ten leagues hence and all their family histories so she knew that what Alice said was true.

"That may be so," she said, "But you have to remember that I am a witch."

Alice, Bella's mother heaved herself from the floor and went to pull the cottage door to. "Don't want no-one repeatin' that load of old imaginings," she grumbled.

"All you have to do, Bella," said Gwen, "is decide what sort of husband you want."

"Handsome, rich and clever," said Bella's mother Alice.

"Aye, but what sort of handsome, what sort of rich and what sort of clever?" said Gwen.

"Bloody handsome, bloody rich and bloody clever," replied Alice.

"I need details for my magic to work," said Gwen, "what sort of man do you like Bella?"

"I like Matthew who works in the top field."

"You like Matthew?" said her mother, "I never knew that! I hope you ain't been doing nothing that you oughtn't. Just wait till I get my hands on that boy."

"Alice stop! The girl's done nothing wrong. She was just answering my question. Now if you could have anything, Bella, what would you have?"

"I would have powder on my face and my hair would be all tarted up on top of my head, and I would ride side saddle on a fine white stallion, and there would be a fire burning in my bedroom all night long."

"What sort of clever would he be?"

"The clever that can talk to me and make me laugh. The clever that is kindhearted and knows what little things give me pleasure."

Here her mother started to grumble again. Gwen hushed her.

"To have all this, my beloved granddaughter, we must go to the river on the night of a storm, stand naked in the water and sing incantations to the moon."

"I ain't getting naked, it's October, I'll freeze to death," said Bella's mother, "you won't catch her a husband, you'll catch her her death."

So some nights later, muffled as best they could be against the cold, with the wind growling around them, they stood on the shore of the river. The lightening seemed to crack the sky in two and great fat raindrops fell through the gaps. All the while Gwen was singing. Even the loudest thunder couldn't manage to mask the sound of her tuneless warbling. And then it was back to the cottage, peeling off wet clothes and shivering in the dark and cold.

"Now you wait and see," said Gwen, "Your man will come to your door and ask for your hand."

"Without seeing her first? How's that gonna come about?" asked Bella's mother.

"Just you wait and see," said Gwen.

Gwen, Bella and Alice waited. They waited through several lambings and harvests and the coldest winters ever seen by mankind. Matthew in the field up yonder got married to a girl who wasn't half the beauty that Bella was. Then one dark and gloomy night when you could only see the flickering faces of those sitting nearest the fire, there was a knock at the door.

The door cracked open and there stood the man of Bella's dreams. Handsome, rich if his clothes were anything to go by, and the light of his eyes said clever.

"I have come to take me a wife," he stated simply. Bella's mother grumbled but Bella simply put on her shawl and walked out into a night so dark that every footfall was like stepping into emptiness. She held the hand of her suitor tightly. It was a cold hand. She rode behind him on a white stallion, rode away from poverty to live with a man who would always have a fire in the hearth, to a future of loving conversations and laughter. Everything was just as Bella wanted it to be, just as Gwen had promised. They married in a small church on the way to his mansion and consummated their nuptials at the first opportunity.

Deep in the darkness of the night Bella awoke and warmed herself before the flames of the fire that made shadows contort and dance in the recesses of the room. The dark tapestries around the bed moved as if alive. She could see the swell of her husband's body. She was so lucky. Bella had the man she wanted, he was handsome, he was rich and he was clever. She walked over to where he lay with the blankets over his head. Bella slipped her hand under the bedclothes to stroke his skin. He was very cold. He stirred, reached out a hand. It was a mighty thin hand with long thick nails. Bella shuddered. He sat up and pulled the blanket away from his face.

Yes, he was handsome, yes he was clever, and yes he was rich. But. But. But. Bella could hardly say it even to herself. She had forgotten to say that her perfect husband should be alive. As he moved she could see the foul threads of sinews that held his bones together, see the leathery deadness of his skin, hear the wheeze of air escaping from his lungs. And now they were married, man and wife together.

Even death would not be able to part them.

A fairy tale ending: the Odd Squad 1

Diana Bretherick

Inspector Anna Lindstrom of Stockholm's police department pulled her jumper over her unruly, cake-filled belly and squinted down at the spectacle before her. The figure of what looked to be an elderly woman was kneeling at her feet. It wore a tweed skirt, sensible shoes and thick stockings. The arms were spread-eagled as if caught in mid flight.

The woman was dead. Anna knew this because the head was stuck in a wood-burning stove and was still smouldering gently in the ashes. The forensic pathologist, Dr Cara Hulten, a tall fierce-looking woman who was crouched beside the body, unfolded her apparently endless limbs and stood up, the plastic of her blue forensics suit crackling.

'Cause of death?' Anna asked.

'Too soon to say for sure.'

'A smoking head is usually fatal, isn't it?' This came from Sven, Anna's partner who was standing near the window in an effort to avoid the smell of burning flesh. She watched him wistfully as he ran his fingers across his unshaven chin. His eyes were still alert despite the dark shadows beneath them. Another late night, no doubt, thought Anna. Oh to be a lithe twenty something again instead of a forty two year old woman who couldn't remember the last time she had seen her feet whilst in a standing position.

Dr Hulten adopted what Sven called her lemon-sucking face. 'It would be difficult to recover from a smoking head, yes. However if you were already dead it would cease to be an issue.'

'I see,' Anna said. 'How long ago?'

'Hard to say exactly, but some time - days rather than hours, I would guess. I'm also guessing...and that's all it is at this point...that again we're looking at some kind of drug being administered. There are injection marks on the side of the neck.'

'Is there anything else you can tell us?'

Dr Hulten paused for a moment and stared at them, a slight smirk on her face, as if she was about to announce the winner of a reality show. 'The victim is not what they seem.'

Anna pulled at her jumper again. Dr Hulten's effortless elegance always made her feel ungainly. 'Go on...Tell me about her. How is she different?'

'She is a he. This is a young man...probably in his early 20s. I'll know more after the post mortem.'

Sven gave a low whistle. 'Cross dressing – curiouser and curiouser!'

'And the body was obviously posed,' Anna said.

Dr Hulten nodded. 'It certainly looks that way.'

Anna thanked her and turned to Sven. 'Did you find anything?'

He held up an evidence bag. 'It was in the left hand...'

'Like the others then...' Anna said. 'What is it? No let me guess... something to do with a fairy tale?'

'Could be...'Sven said. 'It's a piece of candy, shaped like a walking stick. You know – one of those old fashioned ones - stripy.'

Anna looked at it and frowned. 'So which tale are we looking at this time?'

'Hansel and Gretel' Dr Hulten said. 'Our victim is meant to be the witch, I think you'll find.'

'Of course,' Anna said. 'The house made of candy that lured them in. The witch fattened them up for the oven but ended up in there herself.'

'Not in this story,' Sven said, grinning. 'Looks like this witch gave our Hansel more than he bargained for. I wonder what he did to deserve it?'

'We need to establish identity before we think about motive,' Anna said firmly. 'Then we can compare it with the others.' She stared at the corpse. 'I think perhaps it's time to call in an expert.'

The police headquarters in Stockholm was a squat modern place that looked as if it had been thrown at the city rather than built in it. Anna and Sven had been based there for the last six months as part of a new detective unit charged with investigating unusual crimes. Known as the 'odd squad' they were widely regarded as a bunch of eccentrics, thrown together because the force didn't know what else to do with them. The truth was more complex. They had actually been selected for their expertise in different fields. Anna's forte was forensic interviewing and Sven was a not only a tenacious investigator with an impressive arrest record but also specialised in cyber criminology. All this was lost on their colleagues but they used this to their advantage. As Sven put it, 'let them think we're weirdos. At least that way they'll leave us alone.'

As they entered their office, a large untidy room in the basement, Jonsson, the third team member and their resident profiler, held up a piece of paper. 'We've got an ID on the victim,' he announced wearily.

He was, Anna thought, one of the most joyless people she had ever met. For the entire six months that she had known him he had not smiled once. Perhaps that was what came of knowing so much about the criminal mind. An insight into the depths of depravity to which a human being could sink had to be depressing. Jonsson waved the paper at her petulantly. At some point she would have to clarify their respective positions, hers being higher than his. She wasn't looking forward to it. Confrontation was not Anna's thing whereas Jonsson with his flabby bottom, shabby suits, beady little eyes and thin-lipped grimace looked as if he thrived on it. Perhaps she could wear him down by ignoring his hostility. He turned to her, rolled his eyes and waved the paper again. She took it and pinned it to their evidence board whilst Sven mouthed something that looked very like arse, though she couldn't be sure.

Jonsson ignored him. 'Karl Engman, 23 years old, a record as long as the Klarälven river - mostly minor crimes - theft, vandalism, possession of drugs - a regular nuisance in his neighbourhood.'

'Not exactly the same as the others then,' Sven said.

'Did we get hold of Dr Norling?' Anna asked.

Jonsson nodded. 'She's on her way.' He looked at her sceptically. 'Are you sure that a folklore specialist is really what we need?'

'Apparently Dr Norling is much more than that,' Sven said as he peered at his computer. 'It says here that she's an anthropologist with an expertise in criminology and a particular interest in fairy tale narratives. She was consulted on the Robin Hood murders in

Oslo and the Ice Pick killings in Reykjavik.'

'So while we wait for her let's see what we have so far,' Anna said, peering at the evidence board. 'We now have five victims. Toxicology has come back saying that they were all drugged to some degree, probably with a muscle paralytic. All of the bodies were posed and left holding an item, which seems to be an indicator of a fairy tale. First off we have a middle-aged woman, disembowelled, found sitting in a rocking chair, dressed in a red cloak and clutching what looks to be an animal tail.'

'Forensics say it is definitely from a wolf,' Jonsson added. 'A long dead one, it seems.'

'Red Riding Hood,' Sven said.

Anna nodded. 'Yes, an easy one to start with; what do we know about the victim?'

Jonsson rifled through some papers. 'Mary Hult, 43, local politician, lawyer, known for promoting blood sports.'

'Then we have number two,' Anna said, pointing at a photograph of a dark-haired woman with half a wax apple shoved into her mouth. She was wearing a pair of strange metallic shoes.

'Snow White...avenged by the wicked step mother, if I'm not mistaken...' came a voice from the doorway. It belonged to a sturdy, ruddy-faced woman with piercing blue eyes behind a pair of small round wire glasses perched on the end of her nose. Her pale blonde hair was swept back in an untidy pony-tail. She smiled cheerily and strode over to Anna, holding out her hand in greeting. 'I'm Dr Norling.'

Anna shook her hand. It was strange – leathery but oddly soft.

Dr Norling looked at the board intently, going from one photograph to the next and examining it carefully. She muttered under her breath as she did so. 'Yes, yes, how perfect! I see...clever... so very clever.'

'So then, Dr Norling...what do you make of it?' Anna asked.

Dr Norling turned towards her and slowly removed her glasses, blinking as she did so as if she had suddenly emerged into the light from a dark place. 'This is all about revenge,' she said slowly. '... or perhaps more accurately a-venge as it is on behalf of another. It's important to be precise.'

'Go on...'Anna said, intrigued.

'Think of the tales behind these victims…Red Riding Hood eaten by the wolf but freed by a passing woodsman who cut open the wolf and released her. This is the wolf being avenged. Then there's Snow White, poisoned by the wicked step mother who was then made to wear red hot shoes and dance until she dropped dead.'

'I don't remember that in the Disney film,' Sven said.

'Mmm yes…Walt Disney has a lot to answer for,' replied Dr Norling sternly. 'As I said before this is the avenging of the wicked step mother.'

'What about this one?' Anna asked, indicating the photograph of the third victim – a young woman buried up to her thighs in a garden. A second photograph taken from behind revealed an axe buried in the back of her head.

Dr Norling smiled. 'Ah yes…this is one of my favourites… Rumpelstiltskin… more complex than the others. A young woman, whose father falsely claimed that she could spin gold from straw is imprisoned by a King until she has made him a room full of the stuff. If she succeeds he will marry her. If she fails, he will kill her. She cannot do it of course but then an imp creature appears and does it for her in return for her jewellery. But when she can no longer pay him he claims her first born in return for making the rest of the gold. The King marries the girl but the imp returns to claim his prize unless the girl can name him. The girl cannot but tricks him into revealing it himself. Whereupon he is so angry that he stamps his foot hard enough to bury his entire leg up to his waist. Then in a passion he seizes his other foot and tears himself in two.'

'So this is Rumpelstiltskin's revenge…sorry…avenge…' Jonsson said.

'Revenge – that's the noun. As I said, it is important to be precise. You are otherwise correct, right up to the spindle she has in her hand.'

Anna frowned. 'So whoever is doing this is essentially avenging the villains in these stories.'

Dr Norling nodded. 'Yes, clever isn't it?'

'Twisted more like…' Sven said. 'Why would someone do that?'

Anna turned to Jonsson. 'Can you give us a profile?'

He shrugged. 'I suppose so…I've already given it some thought but it will still only be a rough one…'

'Dr Norling...while Jonsson here collects his thoughts, tell us about the last two,' Anna requested.

'With pleasure...' Dr Norling said, licking her lips, clearly relishing the opportunity. 'This one is obviously Cinderella.'

'Obviously?' Anna said. 'How so? The victims' eyes have been put out. I thought the ugly sisters were forgiven by Cinderella.'

'Ah yes...by Cinderella but not by her predecessor in an earlier version of the tale, Aschenputtel. She blinded them in revenge for tormenting her. This is the avenge...I mean revenge... of the step-sisters...and not before time.'

'Fascinating,' Anna said. 'And our latest victim?

'Hansel and Gretel...well Hansel anyway...no doubt Gretel will follow,' Dr Norling said. 'Hansel had his head stuck into the oven by the witch, rather than vice versa. 'The candy is a nice touch. Don't you think?'

'Indeed I do,' Anna said. 'Why don't you have a seat, Dr Norling, while we listen to Jonsson here, give us his profile of the killer?'

Jonsson sighed. 'Like I said, it's only very rough...but we're dealing here with a personality disorder...at the very least...possibly borderline psychotic. This is someone who thinks that their way of seeing the world is the only way.'

'I see and how might we recognise them?' Anna asked.

'They will be intelligent - very well educated - between the age of 30 and 45, with some medical knowledge – or at least access to poisons. And they're angry - furious in fact - at what they see as injustice.'

Anna looked at Dr Norling who was nodding. 'You agree, Doctor?' she asked.

'I do, I do. Injustice is exactly right. In each of these tales a terrible injustice has been done for the sake of a happy ending. The actions of this person are, simply put, the righting of wrongs.' She paused and sighed.

'Go on Doctor,' Anna said.

'In Red Riding Hood the wolf was butchered then, in at least one version of the tale, his body was filled with stones to prevent him from escaping, hence those you found inside the victim.'

'That was more gravel, really,' Sven said.

'Well, it is a matter of symbolism as with many of the tales themselves,' Dr Norling replied. 'In Snow White the so-called 'Wicked Queen' was forced to dance herself to death in red-hot shoes. In Rumpelstiltskin the imp is tormented until he splits himself in half and in Cinderella...the ugly sisters are blinded. Hansel and Gretel murdered the old lady by pushing her into an oven.'

'Self defence, surely!' Sven said, frowning at Anna who was shaking her head at him. 'Wasn't she planning to eat them?'

Dr Norling leapt to her feet. 'No, no, no! Can't you see? They could have run off and called the authorities. But that wasn't good enough for Hansel and Gretel. The witch didn't deserve her fate - none of them did - not really! All of them have been horribly misjudged. They had to be avenged. I have always thought so.'

'Why, Dr Norling?' Anna asked gently. 'Tell us why.'

The academic hesitated for a moment before taking off her glasses and rubbing her eyes. Without them she looked suddenly vulnerable.

'My mother told me versions of these stories when I was a child. She said that they were passed down from mother to daughter so that children could be taught right from wrong. But she also said that there were two ways of looking at every tale and the more I thought about it, the more I could see that she was right. I made it my life's work.' She looked down at her feet. Tears began to fall from her eyes. 'At first it was just an academic pursuit but no one was listening to me. I knew that I had to speak more loudly.'

'And that is when this started, isn't it?' Anna asked, quietly.

Dr Norling sank into a nearby chair and slumped forward, her head in her hands. When she looked up again she was transformed. The vulnerability was quite gone and her eyes glinted with malice.

'All of the victims deserved their fate - Red Riding Hood the hunting supporter so keen on murdering animals, and Snow White had been convicted of elder abuse. Rumpelstiltskin's princess was one of my colleagues at the university, adept at pretending she was more than she was and as a result promoted way beyond her actual abilities.'

'The world is full of people like that,' Jonsson said, looking at Sven.

'And Cinderella?' Anna asked.

'She was just a very unpleasant young woman who I overheard arguing with her sister in a café. And Hansel...I caught him in my own home. He'd broken in. He was a nasty little thug. The world won't miss him.'

'No, but his parents might,' Sven said.

Dr Norling blinked at him. 'I doubt that. In my experience nurture is far more powerful than nature, particularly when it is absent. I was looking out for a Gretel when you called me, Inspector Lindstrom. How could I resist?'

Anna reached for the phone and began to dial. 'I saw you speak at a conference, Dr Norling - a few months ago. There was something not quite right about you and I wasn't the only one to think so.'

'So you invited me in pretending that I was an expert. I suppose that's quite clever.'

Anna shook her head. 'Actually I genuinely thought that you could help us. I just put your oddness down to academic eccentricity.'

'So how...' Dr Norling began.

'You made a simple error Doctor - you started to talk about things that only the killer could know. It was only then that I realised the truth.'

Sven grinned. 'Of course! The spindle in Rumpelstiltskin and Hansel's candy!'

Anna went on. 'You had a message to put across and in the end murder was the only way you could think of to do it. But your arrogance got the better of you.'

Dr Norling nodded slowly. 'It's a shame it has to end like this Inspector. I think you would have made an excellent Gretel.'

'And how would you have despatched me, Doctor?'

The Doctor thought for a moment then a smile spread across her rosy face. 'I would have stuffed you full of sweets and cakes until you burst.'

Anna shrugged. 'I could think of worse ways to go.'

The door opened and two uniformed officers walked in. Dr Norling got to her feet and walked slowly towards them, her hands thrust out in front of her for the handcuffs that one of them was holding. Before leaving she stared at Anna and then gave a mirthless laugh that continued down the corridor as she was led away.

'And they all lived happily ever after,' Sven said.

Anna walked over to the board and began to remove the photographs one by one, ready for the Odd Squad's next case.

The last days of winter

Jacqui Pack

The lacklustre winter sun casts shadows over the terrace of bay fronted houses. A row of lifeless clones, their individual replacement glazing and front doors merely emphasise their similarities. Above the tiled roofs hangs a washed-out sky, existing simply to fill the gap between the earth and the heavens. Only the grey curling smoke of an allotment bonfire interrupts the blanket of banality draped over the street. Its sooty aroma lingers in the air before drifting to the pavement. Winter's early onset stripped the trees bare. Now they stand crucified, awaiting resurrection.

In number Fifteen's magnolia painted spare room, Rose lies on the bed, as if it were a mortuary slab, her body barely disturbing the floral duvet. Her skin is shiny. Like an autumn leaf it crumbles to the touch, the lightest of knocks creating dark stains under its surface. Her skeletal rib cage rises and falls erratically as she breathes through her mouth, rasping as her pain gradually succumbs to medication.

When her failing eyes open they flicker towards the window. Rose is waiting. Her family is waiting. She knows the time will come soon. She closes her eyes and hopes.

Colour. Nothing but colour. Everywhere. Surrounding me, inside of me, so I'm part of it. I don't know how to tell you so as you'll understand the way it is. I've no body to weigh me down, there's just me and the colour. It's exciting, like being out in a summer storm. I feel alive.

All around me are kaleidoscopes of light, gaudy and throbbing; reflections endlessly regenerating, turning and falling, folding in on themselves, repeating; throwing animated rainbow patterns of life around me. I'm made of colour, every possible colour. And all the colours are fresh, like they're newborn.

I can hear colours too. They whisper in my ear like lovers, filling me with vibrations so strong that I can smell and taste them. I know I'm not explaining it properly. It's as if I can taste the hard brightness of the yellow as it shimmers through my eyes; feel the luxury of the red – thick, glutinous, like a velvet trimmed blanket cosseting me. And the black, oh, the black is beautiful. It's got such depth and it shines like a light guiding me. Its brilliance supports me and I really feel as if I'm part of it, as if I'm supporting it too.

Love is a colour, a colour that's everywhere. And colour is music. Have I said that already? And I can rise. I'm soaring into the air, into a crescendo of purple, twirling around, feeling every spiralling note until I reach an orange climax and feel myself shower, like a citrus sea-spray, into the air. I'm everywhere at once and I feel, I feel for the first time complete. Like I'm at home. Back home at last. And the feeling's a sound and a colour and the three overlap and blend until they're all the same and I, I can't really tell you what it's like, except that it's bliss.

Just bliss.

Dark grey clouds gratefully release their cargo. Rain is suspended in the atmosphere, a fine unmoving mist replacing the air. Two cars, professional, sleek, their engines purring discreetly, wait outside number Fifteen. In their uniform blackness they appear more solid than the street with its insipid winter colours.

A small dark-clad group emerges from the house and climbs into the second vehicle. As if choreographed, the two cars move as one, gliding over the tarmac, leaving the street behind.

(Originally published online by The Pygmy Giant, May 2010)

Fresh meat

Alan Morris

The boots swing first one way then another. A moment before they had danced on air scrabbling for a foothold they could not find. Above, a hempen rope creaks like a coffin lid. As the corpse dangles from the gallows tree the crowd disperses, some to taverns, others to brothels a few back to work. The corpse, the focus of so much anticipation, is no longer of interest. At least not for most. But this corpse is not intended to be interred in clay or cast unceremoniously into a lime-filled pit

No, this corpse is for Anatomist Hall: where death delights to aid the living.

Not so much a place as a source of smell - alcohol, abbatoir, a soupçon of the graveyard, hot wax, isinglass, bubbling cauldron. Don't enquire about the contents. Doctors and dissectors armed with lancet probe and saw seek to answer the question, what is life?

How to reignite? Now, that is the question.

Could electricity provide the vital spark?

Mr Grubb calls the meeting to order.

"Today, my friends, will be the decider. Our subject is fresh, almost warm. His limbs still pliant. No sign of corruption or putrefaction yet. Yes very fresh. Fresh meat."

The experiment to revive the dead, is played out upon a stage.

The crowd pay their tuppences and shuffle in; cushions cost a penny extra.

Mr Grubb presides as master of ceremonies.

In the background apparatus hums, sparks fly up.

The corpse sits slumped in the middle of the stage, electrodes attached.

At the back, the assistant cranks the handle.

Grubb gives the signal. "Now!"

The lever is thrown. A jolt. The corpse gasps.

The audience gasps in turn.

Again. The lever is thrown. The corpse opens a baleful eye.

The audience stares back.

Again.

The corpse rises and staggers, arms outstretched, towards the audience.

The audience sways back

Mr Grubb losing control of himself and his experiment produces a lancet and slits the corpse's throat from ear to ear

Future performances are banned.

History does not record whether Mary Shelley was one of those carried fainting from the auditorium.

A final thought as you close your eyes. Don't sleep too long or deep. Remember we are all fresh meat.

Footprints on the lakeside

Justin MacCormack

A long, long time ago, before man began to measure the passage of time, Kal lived in a small cave by the side of a lake. Kal was old, he had survived fourteen summers of his life, and that made him one of the strongest amongst his tribe.

In these days, when the sky was still red for most of the day and the sun was larger than it is today, Kal would spend most of his days hunting on the great veldt for food to bring back to his people. Most of the males in the tribe who were not too young or too old would join him, but Kal was by far the strongest amongst them, for he could wrestle any of the thickly-haired gazelles to the ground without hurting himself. And when the sharp-toothed creatures that stalked in the night came to the caves to feed, Kal would fight them off with his sharpened sticks and cutting stones. Kal wore the skin of one of the night creatures to conceal his nakedness, and lined the floor of his caves with other pelts to keep him warm at night.

It was the day after the old one had died. Kal had no language, and did not have a name for the word 'father', but he did understand that the old one was important to him in some strange and indistinct way, and had done his best to ensure that this old one was fed before the other elders of the tribe. The old one had perished slowly, having been bitten by a creature that would one day be recognised as a snake, but its teeth had been sharp and edged with a poison that had steadily infected the old one until his ankle had swollen and left him unable to walk.

Kal had seen others die before, falling to the teeth of those that stalked the night, but he found himself uncertain what to do now that the old one had died. The sun was dipping low in the sky when

Kal decided what he should do for the old one. Taking great care, Kal gathered one of the skins of a night creature that he had slain from the floor of his cave, and wrapped it around the old one's body. Then, carefully, he lifted the body and walked down from the hillside towards the lake.

The lake sat at the foot of the hill, with a small trail of shale stones that lead down to it from the caves. Kal stepped cautiously, knowing that if he went too quickly the stones of the trail to the lake would cut his bare feet. The lake itself was a thing of curiosity to the tribe, for it was the source of the water that they drank each day. There was no other water for many days' walk, and so the tribe had lived here by this lake for years beyond memory. Kal kneeled down next to the lakeside, and placed the old one's body beside the water. Looking out into the lake, Kal watched as its surface shimmered slightly in the red sunlight, the waters looking to be a hot orange-red hue. At times, the water seemed to sway and move slightly, almost as if on its own volition.

Kal was more curious about the water than many of the tribe. There were many of the women folk who would not approach the lake, concerned with the way its colour would change, growing from a sombre orange to shimmering silver during the times when the sun was at its highest in the sky or into blackness when the night crept out. Kal knew that small creatures would move through the water, little silver things with large eyes which one day his descendants would learn to catch, but that day was far away.

All Kal understood was that when he grew thirsty, he came to the lake and drank its waters, and because he had to do this several times on each day he had the sense that the lake was somehow important. Crouching on his haunches, Kal removed the pelt that wrapped the old one's body and slung it over his shoulder. He looked at the old one's body once more, in the orange-red light of the setting sun. The lake seemed indifferent to the old one, its ripples licking softly at its shore. Kal stood and walked back to his cave.

The next morning rose and the tribe gradually awakened. The things that stalked the night had not tried to feed whilst they had slept, but Kal and the other strong hunters of the tribe always slept with their sharp stones or sticks close at hand. Gradually they chewed on the remaining berries that they had scavenged the day before, and emerged from their caverns into the dawning sunlight.

As with each morning, the tribe took their exodus down the little shale-marked trail to the side of the lake to quench their nightly thirst. They sat and crouched and leaned on the lakeside, cupping their hands into the waters and holding palmfuls to their mouths, drinking eagerly, but none of the tribe would venture to swim in the waters. Not even Kal, whose lithe body was strong enough to surely keep afloat, would dare to try, for none of them could guess how deep the lake was.

As he crouched by the lakeside, drinking in heavy gulps, Kal looked out into the lake and watched the soft ripples from far out on the lake. On the far side, Kal could see other creatures that lived on the veldt as they came to drink from the lake, sitting on the opposite edge of the waters to keep distance from Kal and the tribe, who they recognised as their hunters.

Gradually, Kal grew to realise that the old one's body was no longer resting on the edge of the waters. This did not disturb Kal, as in those days, time was reckoned differently than it is now, and what had happened on the last day was as distant as a hundred years hence. Even so, the memory of having left the old one by the lakeshore dwindled lightly in Kal's mind, with a sense of similarity that was familiar to him. Just as he had left his sharp stone by the pelt he slept under when he slept that night, he had left the old one here, by the side of the lake.

The bank of the lake was edged with a material that was wet and muddy beneath Kal's toes, and if the hunter were to dig down far enough, he would be able to find handfuls of clay. The muddy banks often dried in the sunnier seasons, leaving the ground cracked and brown. As Kal wandered from the rest of his tribe so that he could look around the area where he had left the old one, he found a large number of footprints in the mud of the bank.

Kal was a hunter, and as such he recognised that when he was tracking a gazelle, the marks they left on the ground could show the direction that his prey had travelled. Kal knew his own footprints, wet as they were in the mud, and he recognised that these other footprints in the mud were not his own. The tribe rarely travelled so far along the lakeside, preferring to stay near the trail that lead back up to the caves. A sense of uncertainty stirred within Kal, a feeling he had rarely experienced, and he felt that it tasted bitter to him.

Circling around the footprints, Kal tried to determine how many of the footprints there were. This was always difficult to do, and it was a great skill of a hunter to recognise the difference between 'few' and 'many', as many prey could be dangerous even to a group of hunters armed with the sharpest of stones. But Kal could not tell how many had walked here where the old one had been laid, because the footsteps trampled over one another.

A realisation gripped Kal in that moment, causing the faint little hairs on his arms and neck to bristle. The footprints were not those of his tribe, for they did not venture out this far. Indeed, as he looked back, he noticed that many of his tribe were making their way back up along the shale trek to prepare for the day's hunt, with only him remaining. He crouched down on his haunches and tried to see more of the footprints, realising that they were not the tracks of a gazelle, or even a large cat with their sharp teeth that stalk through the night. It looked almost like his own footprints, with five toes and heel strong in the mud, but not quite the same.

Kal wanted to track them, to find who had come so close to the lake. He wanted to protect the caves where his people slept, the lakes in which they drank. Kal knew that his tribe was not alone on the veldt, that other tribes lived elsewhere across the Great Plains. They had their own water, their own creatures to hunt for food, and in those days they had not yet had any need to fight over space. Kal remembered a time, many summers ago, when another tribe had travelled far to claim the caves as their own and the women folk as their breeding stock, and been fought off by the tribe's strongest warriors. Now Kal was the strongest warrior, and so he was the best to fight any others who came to claim the caves or the lake or the women folk.

Following in a series of long, circling steps, Kal moved around the footsteps on the lakeside to track where the strange others had come from and where they had gone. If they were close, Kal could move the others to attack first, before the strange others had the chance. Kal would claim their food and add their women folk to the tribe. The footsteps did not move away from the lake. In fact, they seemed to originate from the water, loop and stagger back and forth around the ground where the old one had been laid down, and then descend back into the lake's silvery surface.

It was a good, strong gazelle, and it had given a strong hunt.

Kal had brought it down during the day, when the sun had been at its highest. He and three other hunters had tracked the young gazelles across the fields distant from the lake, pursuing them eagerly. The taste of meat was a significant temptation, rarer as it was than the taste of berries which the hunting party would usually bring back to the caves.

The gazelles had been grazing when the hunters had sprung, moving close by keeping downwind of the prey. By the time that the gazelle had become aware of the hunters, it had been too late. The group had broken into the herd and brought down two of the younger bucks, piercing their flanks with their sharpened sticks, cutting at their legs and throats with their stones.

Two young bucks would feed the tribe for the next couple of days, but Kal broke from the party and sprang eagerly to bring down a third gazelle, a fully-grown adult male. The decision to do so was not unnoticed among the other hunters, as one of the others turned and gave an angered cry at Kal. It was a foolish decision, as the male gazelle could lash out with a kick strong enough to break a bone, and Kal was fortunate not to fall victim to this. Instead he managed to grapple atop the creature, driving the sharpened edge of his stone into the gazelle's skull again and again, driving it twitching down to the ground.

Kal lay on the ground beside the gazelle and caught his breath. The male who had barked at him angrily approached, his barks continuing and edged with a sharp snarl. Kal recognised the other male; it was one who lived also among the caves. The people did not use names, not as they are recognised today, but the sound that others made when they wanted to indicate this male was 'Tak'. Tak kicked the gazelle, and struck it roughly with his stone. His intention was clear. He was angry; his snarl told Kal that his choice to break from the hunt had put the others in jeopardy. It would have been easy for one of the gazelle to have cut through a hunter with their sharp horns. Tak thumped the gazelle with his stone again. "You are weak and stupid" he was indicating, "And I wish to take this food from you."

Kal leapt to his feet, barking loudly at Tak. Clutching his own sharp stone in his hand, he lunged a step towards the other male. Tak hurried back a step, and both males looked coldly at each other. Kal waited, watching to see what Tak would do. Gradually, Tak stepped back. Kal watched the other male lope steadily back to the group.

The gazelle had to be carried between two of the hunters, which lengthened their time in getting back to the caves with a slow trek, and by the time they got home the sun was already starting to descend in the sky. The tribe gorged on the meat that night, enjoying the freshness of the food and the strength it brought to their bodies.

But with the wealth of gazelle that the hunters had brought back, the tribe were too gorged to devour the bulk of the adult male. As the sun dipped beneath the crimson horizon and the stars began to fill the sky, Kal dragged the half-eaten bulk of the gazelle down from the mouths of the caves. He pulled it along the shale path that lead down, tugging it in weary jerks until he finally arrived at the side of the lake's pitch-black surface.

The pelt wrapped around Kal's shoulders kept the cold bite of the night at bay. He sat at the mouth of the cave, clutching his sharp stone to his chest, watching the black lake.

The lake had been there since Kal was a mere child, since before he could remember. It had always been there, it was a constant. Always there, sitting in silence, just beyond his doorstep. Kal did not look up, did not gaze into the starlit sky as his descendants would. He gave no thought to the large pale moon that hung high above him, bathing the veldt in the light he needed to see in the night's darkness. In the untold years and ages to come, Kal's children's children would look up into the sky. But for now, Kal looked down, into the black waters of the lake, impossibly deep, unfathomably empty, and unknowably infinite.

He had kept his stone tight, running his fingers along it. It had, over many summers of use, been perfected. It was carved to a point on one side, with one corner of that point being sharp – sharp enough to cut through the skin of the gazelle. Or, he hoped, the leather of the strange others who intruded into his tribe's home.

If Kal had possessed much in the way of memory, he would have thought about the stone that he held. He had used it many times to bring down the larger creatures, so that he could bring food back to the caves. He had chased some from the mouths of the caves when things in the night had come to claim his people as food of their own. And once, some summers ago, Kal had almost turned the stone on one of his fellow cave-dwellers who had grown jealous of the female that Kal had chosen to mate with, and wanted to claim the female for his own. The cave-dwellers existed only in the present, barely able to recall the past or look towards the future; but in the dim recesses of his mind, Kal could still recognise the face of the jealous challenger every time he looked upon Tak.

Kal struggled to resist the urge to sleep; the chill of the night forced him to pull the pelts around him closer. He had not even recognised that he had been laying a trap for the strange others, with their weird footprints so indistinctly different from his own, slightly more broad, toes slightly longer.

When the urge of sleep started to tug its hardest at Kal and he found his shoulders slouching, his eyelids closing and his grip on his stone loosening, it was the sound of the movement of the lake's surface that brought Kal sharply to attention.

Reflecting in the moon's light, the black surface of the lake shimmered with silvery ripples. Kal's eyes snapped open, and he lowered himself closer to the floor of the cave. As he watched, the ripples started to spread outwards, sending wide circles across the water. Gradually, the source of the ripples began to move, working their way closer towards the shore. The young hunter started to make his way towards the shale path, keeping his body as low to the ground as he could, ready to catch the strange others unaware.

The surface of the lake broke as the beings' heads emerged from the dark waters into the moonlit night. The moonlight reflected against the damp surface of their flesh, vibrant against the liquid's eternally bleak shade. The figures emerged slowly, their heads turning to survey the lakeside – yes, Kal was sure; there were three of the beings. What hair they had was long and coated flat to the curves of their skulls in thick rope-like strands. Their features were sharp, as precise as the razor-edged stone that Kal clutched frantically in his fist. Their noses were short and close to their faces, but narrow and looking almost straight, as were their brows. Where on Kal's head sat his ears, the creatures had nothing but smooth skin, concealed by wet tangles of hair. Their bodies were tall, taller than Kal or any in the tribe, and as thin and precise as their features; their arms were long, as were their legs, elongated and pointed in jointed elbows. Their hands, like the feet that made the footprints upon the mud of the lakeside, were broad, flat and long. They wore nothing but the water's glistening reflection of the moon's light on their bodies, and as they moved they stepped in uncertain, slouching steps, as if unfamiliar with the very ground beneath their feet.

More than anything else, though, Kal could not help but notice the shade of their skin, which seemed unlike any colour he had seen at once before. It seemed as dark as the lake at night and as blue as the waters at midday, as orange as the sky at sundown, and as silver as the light from the moon, all at the same time.

The three beings canted their heads to one another, as if in communication, turning their gaze from one another to the lump of gazelle on the lakeside. They stood for a while there, as though reaching a decision, when Kal finally tried to move closer, his foot sifting quietly against the shale.

One of the creatures turned and looked directly at Kal.

The young hunter stopped where he was. He looked back at the creature, as its two companions turned to view the young man from the cave, dressed in his furs. And that was when Kal saw the one thing that he would remember for the rest of his days.

The creatures had the most beautiful eyes.

The next day would dawn, and Kal would still think of the creatures with the beautiful eyes. He would remember them dragging the gazelle back down from the lakeside, with their long, thin fingers. He would remember the creatures sliding into the lake's infinite, unknowable embrace with the ease of a child nestling against their mother's breast. He would remember checking the ground where the creatures had come ashore, and finding only their peculiar footprints at the lakeside.

But more than anything else, he would remember that they had the most beautiful eyes.

And so it was that on the next day, Kal brought down another gazelle, and left it on the banks of the lake for the creatures to claim. He did so on the third day as well, hoping that the creatures would accept what he brought to them. That night however, as Kal sat near-slumbering at the mouth of the cave, he noticed another figure skulking its way along the lakeside.

It wasn't until he was halfway down the shale path that Kal recognised the figure as Tak. The other male stood in the moonlight, towering above the dead gazelle at the side of the lake. Keeping low against the shale, Kal watched as Tak, who so many months ago had challenged Kal for the female to mate with, and challenged him only a few days ago on his rights to hunt, stood ready to challenge those unknown things that accepted Kal's offerings at the lakeside.

Tak stood fully upright, his body painted in the silver light of the moon. He wore no furs to slow his movement, he was here to fight. He slammed the stone he held against the offered gazelle, and with a sturdy kick he sent the body trailing in the dust, rolling away from the corner of the lake. He turned to Kal and bellowed, mockingly. 'See what I have done to you and your lake friends', he seemed to say. 'You are unfit to lead. The tribe is mine'.

Anger bubbled inside Kal. The other male was not simply challenging him - that was something he could have easily resolved in a fight. Instead he felt as if something far more important was being threatened; something intangible and unspeakable, as if the creatures with the beautiful eyes would have grown enraged with Tak as well. He had insulted them, and that made Kal's rage churn and seethe inside him. He ran forward, and made to strike the arrogant male who stood in defiance not just to Kal, but to the unknowable things that lurked within the infinite depths of the abyssal lake.

His strike knocked Tak backwards, causing him to stumble. He hit Tak again and again, Kal's sharp stone growing wet and slippery as it drew wounds into Tak's body. In the moonlight, the cuts leaked with the same shade of liquid as the lake itself. Tak's feet gave out beneath him, and he fell into the waters, snarling all the meanwhile at Kal.

And it was there that the creatures seized him. The hands, thin and elongated, burst from the surface of the water and wrapped around Tak's legs. Another pair grasped his shoulders, and their glistening claws scraped along his skin. Tak struggled, desperately. He tried to pull himself back up, urging himself back to land, searching for it frantically with his hands like a blind man.

Within only a few seconds, Tak slipped beneath the surface of the water. His face remained, wet and shining in the moonlight above the black eternity of the lake, before the creatures with beautiful eyes took that down into the depths with them as well. The creatures feasted well that night, and for all the nights after.

In the days that followed, Kal would set aside a part of each hunt. Each evening, when the rest of the tribe were asleep, he would bring the gazelle, some days it would be antelope, or if the tribe had hunted especially well, even part of a buffalo. When the tribe did not have such good fortune in their hunts, he would bring berries, or fruits. Each morning, Kal would return to find that what he had left was gone. And when one of the tribe would die, he would take their body to the side of the lake, from where the person had drank the waters all their life, and return the next day to find that the body had returned into the embrace of the lake.

In time, Kal would teach his own children to do the same, and they would in turn teach their children. Kal, and none of his descendants, would understand what an offering was; such concepts were foreign to them and would continue to be so for many ages. And when Kal was an old man, he knew that he too would be brought down to the lake by his children.

For all the rest of his days until then, though, Kal never again saw the creatures with beautiful eyes. But each morning, he would see their footprints on the lakeside.

Ghost

V H Leslie

The water hadn't been clean since Fergus died. The pond filter had stalled that very week, its rotary apparatus refusing to turn as if in silent protest for Fergus' passing. Annette had been far too busy arranging the funeral to be concerned with the small matter of a defective motor. And afterward she had to contend with the solicitors, the bills, the pension scheme, on top of her three daughters – all grown but somehow children again since the loss of their father – crying into her apron as if they were smaller than her and not the other way around. Annette envied the faulty filter, wishing that she could just stop dead as Fergus had. But she had to keep going, getting up each morning to propel their lives forward, ensuring that their little world continued to turn.

Only much later, when she'd cast off her mourning duties, did she notice how murky the water had become. The pond was little more than a large begonia-rimmed smudge across the lawn. She peered into the gloomy depths wondering if her neglect had affected any of the pond's inhabitants. But the muddied surface gave nothing away. If life existed at all it was in the dark. She reached for the net that was balanced across the back of a ceramic tortoise; left there from the last time Fergus had used it. Long idle judging from the accretion of leaves lining the mesh. She shook it clean and plunged it deep.

It was like a lucky dip, these blind sweeping motions through the water, only to be rewarded with a brimful of algae. She picked out the woolly clumps and drove the net in deeper. The only thing that was clear was that nothing could live in such a stagnant pool.

A flick of silver and the brief shimmer of fish scales contradicted her. And then it was gone. The bobbing water as the ripples receded was the only clue that something had been there at all. So there was life in the old gal yet. Annette waited until the water settled and returned indoors.

Every one agreed that the pond was in an alarming state. Her daughters complained of the dank smell and they ushered their children away from it as if it were contagious. Why don't you pave it over, Mum, they said. It would make a lovely patio area. You could get that hammock you always wanted.

The pond had been Fergus' province. Annette didn't know the first thing about maintaining it. She had no understanding or desire to understand the specialist equipment, the maintenance regimes and checks, the disease prevention measures which Fergus had detailed so meticulously in various notebooks and manuals. It would be too much upkeep for a woman of her age. Her daughters had all married partners as ineffectual as they were. None of them wanted to take on Fergus' legacy. None of them was prepared to get their hands dirty. It was easier to cover it over and start again.

She didn't tell them about the fish she'd seen, the one she'd glimpsed numerous times since. It would only complicate matters. People were overly sentimental about pets. Let them believe nothing existed in those dark depths. The pond had become so congested with silt and leaves, clogged with blanketweed, that it was easy to think that life within had just given up. Preferable in fact, than the idea that something dwelled in those black and putrid waters.

But life subsisted. Annette watched a solitary fin skirt the surface, hovering there as if to afford a better view, its milky, almost translucent colouring vaguely familiar. She recalled the times spent at pet shops and leisure centres where koi enthusiasts would display their fish in the shallow confines of paddling pools or tanks. She could see Fergus immersed in this exotic world of colour, selecting the best on offer, the babies mostly – cheaper and more likely to be disease free – to be netted and bagged. On the journey home, the girls, children then, would each clutch a plastic bag, relishing the spongy weight in their laps as the fish turned circles in their transparent worlds. And they'd christen them with silly names, Gillian, Fishfinger, Jaws, which they forgot as they got older, as they became more interested in life beyond the back garden.

Annette found carp pretty unmemorable too, all except one, on account of his cloudy anaemic colouring, the shadowy patterning along his belly and sides so that his dorsal fin stood out white and skeletal. A ghost koi, which the girls had rather un-inspiringly named Ghost.

It was Ghost that remained now, Annette was sure of it. Solitarily haunting what was left of the pond.

The possibility of moving him to another pond wasn't an option. She had a vague memory of his having contracted some kind of carp disease. A disease that had made his body swell, forcing his eyes to bulge outwards. His skin developed a milky film of mucus that seemed to encircle him like ectoplasm, making his name even more appropriate. Perhaps she remembered the fish so well because of her husband's repeated attempts to treat him. He had been relegated to the children's paddling pool more than once, in makeshift quarantine while her husband administered homemade remedies or drugs recommended by other fanatics. She'd found Ghost once, floating lifeless on his side, as if dead. And she'd been somewhat relieved that this sickly fish had finally kicked the bucket, freeing her husband from further toil, only for him to suddenly revive and dart off into the depths. Perhaps he wasn't sick at all, just indolent.

Ghost rose now to the surface. His huge suction mouth gulping at the air. The barbels either side resembling a drooping moustache. He looked whiter, strangely more translucent, visible only because the water was so dark, so murky. Had the water been as clean as Fergus would have liked, Ghost may have disappeared altogether. That was what she wanted. Why couldn't he have just died in the paddling pool all those years ago? Annette felt a stab of guilt, but let him swim free with thoughts of her new patio. She'd already selected the hammock she wanted from the catalogue, complete with stripy awning and drinks holder. Her dreams were finally becoming more concrete and she wasn't going to let some ailing phantom get in her way.

So she'd tried in her subtle way to engineer his death. She removed the plastic heron, which stood sentinel-like from the top of the shed and even sprinkled bird feed next to the pond – an open invitation for nature to attack tooth and claw. But the birds refused to make a meal of him, as did the neighbour's cats, which avoided the pond as if sensing Ghost's unnatural existence, his strange abnormal longevity. If only something could finish him off. She'd begun to feed him less and less, and now she'd stopped altogether, hoping that she could starve him out. She tried to think of it as a kindness. To live in such darkness could only mean to suffer. She knew that in time, without clean, properly oxygenated water, the pond would become ripe with disease. Wouldn't it be better to hasten it along, than to draw it out any longer than was necessary?

Fergus had hung on as well. Much longer than anyone had expected. When he was brought home it was because everyone knew there was no hope. The treatments and drugs had all failed; they couldn't stop his inevitable decline. So he was tucked up in his own bed, to live out his final days with his family. But Fergus didn't seem to get the memo. He refused to comply with the doctors and nurses, the specialists and their expert prognoses. He just wouldn't roll over and die. Instead, the bedroom became a stagnant holding pen, Annette's linen took on the odour of death and she and the girls became as pallid and ashen as Fergus was. Living ghosts, while Fergus kept his head above water and swelled and burgeoned, fed with drugs and fluids by matronly carers. Initially, he tried to haul himself out of bed, but his arms were too frail. She'd watch as her daughters clasped his hands, hands that had once relished the handiwork around the bungalow, hands that had served the pond so diligently, now swollen and ineffectual. Near the end he couldn't speak. Communication was reduced to the most basic of exchanges. Blink once for yes, twice for no. His lashes would flutter lightly in obedience, while he lay there day after day, immobile, listless.

*

That night Ghost swam into Annette's dreams. The pond was a dark shadow illuminated by the solar powered spotlights Fergus had installed around its periphery. A deep black hollow, an open sore across their otherwise perfect lawn. Surely nothing could live in such a place. A cluster of white buds, translucent like frogspawn, broke the surface. They floated there a moment but then reared upwards like mushroom stalks, reaching into the dark night, until they stopped suddenly and drooped forward as if exhausted by the enterprise. Then Annette realised what she was seeing. Fingers. Long, anaemic fingers which groped at the paving slabs, and pushed against them to haul the rest of it – whatever it was – from the depths. Amid the dark and the splashing, she could see flashes of white, the metallic shimmer of fish scales and long wiry barbels licked the air.

She watched the strange hybrid scurry out of the pond, with hands where its dorsal fins should be, walking on fingertips across the lawn, towards the house. In her dream, she saw herself sleeping soundly, while the strange white spectre crept towards the bed, gripping the sheets with its long ghostly fingers, pulling its scaly wet bulk up onto the pillow beside her. She watched as the long fingers curled over the top of the bed sheets, reaching out towards her, with its gulping fish mouth, those snaking barbels, moving closer and closer.

The bed was soaked through when she finally woke up. Her body was still clammy and feverish as she pulled off the sheets and carried them through to the washing machine. She was relieved when her daughters arrived later that day, a large cardboard box in tow. Whilst Annette made the tea, the girls opened it, strewing the contents across the lawn. Annette glimpsed the stripy upholstery, green like the algae that festered along the rim of the pond. While her daughters argued over the self-assembly instructions, Annette encouraged the children to throw stones into the pond. There's nothing in there, she told them as she filled their palms with pebbles.

Maybe that was the truth. In her dream, Ghost had pulled himself out of the water and left the pond behind. Was that how it had been all those millions of years ago, when our piscine antecedents had pulled themselves out onto land? Had we all emerged from a form of pond life? And did those creatures have hands too, or had they just dragged themselves upon fat fins, tossing and rolling themselves forward because it was better than staying where they were?

Annette could understand that. Why would anything want to stay in such a dark place? She remembered how upset Fergus had been a few years before, when a couple of koi had leapt from the pond. The nitrate levels had been too high, inducing suicidal tendencies. Of course the fish didn't know it was suicide, Annette had argued. To them, the unknown was a better option than a long, drawn out death. It was actually a leap of faith. What she couldn't understand though, was why they hadn't all jumped, why some stayed behind and tolerated those toxic levels. Why some would always linger at the bottom of the pond and persist in the darkness.

The children had made a game of throwing stones and now ran at the pond like shot-putters with larger slabs they'd acquired from the rockery. If Ghost hadn't left on his own accord, they were actively prompting his exorcism. Her unknowing assassins. Annette heard her daughters cheer as they lifted the hammock upright, one of them gently pushing the swing seat. Her attention was only away from the pond for a moment but when she turned back her grandson was at the pond's edge, and a white fin was cutting through the black water.

She saw it all as she rushed towards her grandson, the milky hand rising up out of the water as it had in her dream, clasping his little ankle and pulling him down into the murky depths, where he'd remain forever, turning circles and blowing bubbles that would break pitifully on the surface. She said as much to her daughters, who led her inside with alarmed looks, guiding her towards her bed and fetching aspirin. The grandchildren, bewildered but unharmed, continued with their game, filling the pond with rocks.

*

The hammock sat on the lawn beside the pond. The upholstery was darker, saturated from the rain. Annette hadn't been outside to place the tarpaulin cover over it. In fact, she'd hardly been out at all, confined to the house since her strange episode in the garden. She tried to keep herself busy, but the housework only took so long. She couldn't bear idle hands so she made her way to the bedroom and sat down on the freshly laundered sheets. She picked up a pillow and held it to her face. She thought she'd gotten rid of it, but it was still there, lingering in the background. The smell of death. She stripped the linen and carried the bundle to the washing machine. Kneeling on the floor, she watched the sheets go round in the drum. A white blur. She had to keep her world turning, she reasoned. Her bright, sanitary world.

After she'd tumble-dried the sheets, she ironed them. There was something enjoyable about prolonging these small tasks. She never had the time when the girls were young. How they would interrupt her chores, get under her feet as she made the beds, placing the sheets over their heads with warbling cries, Woooo, woooo, playing ghosts.

She'd had her fill of ghosts. The one that disturbed her most haunted a little over four feet of water. They'd existed in this strange stalemate for too long already. She moved to the window and looked out at the pond. The water was dark, motionless. Perhaps she was finally free of Ghost.

She made her way out into the garden, surprised at the alarming growth of her wisteria, the rebellious borders. The pond's surface was covered in a sickly crust of algae and pondweed like the membrane of a scab. She reached for the net, still balanced on the back of the ceramic tortoise and drove it into the water.

There was nothing but pond debris and leaves. At first she was cautious but then she swept the net through the water blindly, without hesitation. It couldn't do more damage than the rocks the grandchildren had deposited so violently into the water. She was beginning to sense victory, when the net pulled and she felt a weight at the end of the stick.

As she lifted Ghost from the water, she was reminded of Fergus, without his dentures, gulping air from his wide toothless mouth. The drugs had given his skin a translucent quality, a wet slickness, though the skin itself had dried, making his eczema more pronounced, the skin flaking off into the bed sheets where it accumulated in clumps like shavings of parmesan. Blink once for yes, twice for no, the girls had chorused, encouraging him to answer their inane questions.

When they were alone, Annette didn't engage in any form of communication. She was sick of his inert body, lifeless except for his eyes, which followed her around the room, blinking hard to get her attention. She wanted to close them. She wanted her bed back, the sheets clean, free of disease. She ran her hand on the pillow beside him, recalling the children beneath the white sheets. Ghosts.

She lifted Ghost free of the water, his body curled within the net like a white flag. She watched him unfurl and loll against the mesh, struggling for breath, his gills labouring. She saw the scaly, metallic surface of his skin, the patina of mucus, interrupted by numerous ulcerous cavities, inflicted probably from the barrage of stones and pebbles. She could identify the onset of disease – recalling images from Fergus' books – in the curvature of Ghost's spine, the pine-coning of his tail. His scales fanned outwards, his fins rotten and torn, trailing behind him like ribbons.

Now will you die? Annette thought, turning the net towards her, looking into the face of her adversary. But there, above his bulging eyes, two fleshy flaps hung loose. Was this some strange new growth, a leprous protuberance? If Annette didn't know better, she'd have said they were eyelids. Holding him aloft, she saw her reflection in his black pupils, could sense him regarding her from behind white-lidded eyes.

And he blinked twice.

Blood will tell: the Odd Squad 2

Diana Bretherick

Harry Hartmann settled down into his tatty armchair in the museum's tiny office and put his newspaper over his face. Security was largely optional as far as he was concerned. They paid him a pittance and he responded by doing his job in the sort of half-hearted way that, in his mind at least, it deserved. Still it wasn't just about the money, despite what his wife said. Christmas was coming and it wasn't cheap. Lisbeth always wanted the best, whether they could afford it or not. She had been absolutely livid when he'd told her that he'd taken this over the factory job, which would have paid more. But who wants to be stuck in an empty factory when you could wander at will round a museum full of curiosities? It was just as well his brother Anders had backed him up. 'Wasn't there such a thing as job satisfaction?' he'd said when Lisbeth had complained at a family dinner. And Harry did enjoy his job, for all his grumbling. It gave him a sense of purpose and besides he had a kind of affinity with the exhibits.

True they had spooked him a bit when he first started. When he did his tour of duty round the various rooms he sometimes thought that he could hear movement, as if the ghosts from Scandinavia's colourful criminal past were stalking him. Anyone who thought that Nordic life was one big peace party would soon realise that was just one big myth after a couple of hours viewing the extensive collection at Stockholm's Museum of Crime.

The CCTV flickered slightly giving out a ghostly grey light, but Harry was oblivious as he began to slip inexorably into his regular evening doze.

Then, something made him wake. He started and his newspaper fell to the ground. He blinked blearily at the screens. At first he thought something had just fallen over. There didn't seem to be much going on in the museum. Then he saw it. A figure in what looked to be a hooded cloak – not the usual burglar's garb – was moving across hall one – 'The History of Capital Punishment'. Harry sprung to life and made towards the relevant room. It wasn't every day he got to apprehend a real criminal. He might even get a pay rise.

He moved quietly through the grisly exhibits – nooses, chains, weapons and various instruments of torture – his skin prickling with anticipation. He paused for a moment. Was that something rustling? He walked slowly towards the sound. There it was again –not rustling but breathing. He inched forwards and then out of the corner of his eye he saw a curtain twitch. He braced himself, holding his own breath...but then it moved again and as he got nearer Harry could see that it was just a breeze through an open window. He exhaled with relief and went to shut the window, cursing under his breath whoever had left it open. He turned round and stopped again, just to be sure, but he couldn't see or hear anything untoward and he started to think that the cloaked figure was just a left-over from his dreams. Then suddenly it became only too clear to Harry that far from being a remnant of his unconscious world, it was all horribly and painfully real.

As the axe went crashing through his neck for the first time, he wished that he'd taken the factory job after all.

Inspector Anna Lindstrom viewed the scene with her usual detached curiosity. When she had first been told about the crime she had doubted that it was really a case for her 'odd squad', the nickname at Stockholm police station for her small unit of specialist police officers tasked specifically to deal with unusual crimes. She couldn't see what was so unusual about the murder of a security guard at a museum in the course of a theft. Unpleasant, yes but something of an occupational hazard surely and certainly not weird or strange. Her viewpoint had changed however since she learned that the mode of death was decapitation and that both the murder weapon, one of the exhibits, and the head of the unfortunate victim, were missing.

She shifted uncomfortably in her forensics suit and wished it was bigger and she was smaller. Her colleague Sven was peering over the shoulder of Kaspar, their forensics specialist as he examined the case where the murder weapon, an axe, had originated. Kaspar, a dapper young man with a short clipped beard and small rimless glasses perched precariously on the end of his nose, turned round and glared at him. 'Do you have to get so close? I can smell your after shave and it isn't a pleasant experience!'

Sven held his hands up in capitulation. 'Sorry...just trying to get a full picture...Anyway what's wrong with my after shave – its Aramis!'

Kaspar shook his head. 'Yeah well you keep telling yourself that friend, if it makes you feel better.'

Anna tutted. 'Never mind his aftershave...what can you tell me?'

'Not much, I'm afraid. The glass was broken with a blunt instrument of some kind. There's no blood or any other traces. Forensically there's zilch, I am afraid.'

'Great,' Anna muttered and looked towards Dr Cara Hulten, the forensic pathologist, who was kneeling elegantly beside the headless body as if she was doing a little light gardening. 'Anything?'

'I can shed a little more light...but not much more at this stage,' she said. 'The first cut is clean but it took more than one. It certainly wasn't a pleasant death, if there is such a thing. We're definitely looking at an axe. That much I can be sure of. But it doesn't look as if it had been sharpened recently.'

Kaspar gulped and ran his hand across his throat.

'Not just any axe...' announced Sven. Anna suppressed a smile. Her partner's sense of drama came from his student membership of the Malmo University Dramatic Society or MUDS as it had been affectionately known. She pretended to be disapproving at times like this but somehow it made their job, which was almost always a dark one, a little easier to bear.

'Go on. I know you're dying to tell us...'

Sven grinned as everyone else groaned. 'Well I don't think it's a coincidence that an axe was taken. It was used to execute a namesake of yours, Anna Mansdottur, back in 1890. She and her son Pers Nilsson murdered his wife, Hanna Johannsdottur. Mother and son were having an incestuous relationship. He got a life sentence but was released in 1914.'

'Interesting. I wonder why he escaped execution and she didn't. It hardly seems fair...' Anna mused.

Dr Hulten cleared her throat. 'I hate to interrupt but have you searched the rest of the museum?'

'Not yet,' Anna replied. 'Why?'

Dr Hulten languorously got to her feet and pointed to the far corner of the room. 'I don't think the axe was the only thing to go missing.'

Back at the station, in their basement HQ, the Odd Squad, Anna, Sven, Kaspar and the profiler Jonsson gathered to consider the evidence, not that there was much.

'This is more a question of what we don't have, rather than what we do,' Anna said, looking at the photographs of the missing artefacts. 'We need to go through each and consider their significance to see if they tell us anything. Sven, you do the honours.'

'We know about the axe. But also missing was a torn piece of sheeting used by a woman called Hilda Nilsson, also known as the 'angel maker'. She was sentenced to death for the murder of several young children but hanged herself with the bed sheet in her jail cell.'

'Any relation to Pers Nilsson?' Jonsson asked.

'Not as far as I can make out,' Sven replied. 'But get this...also taken was a book of spells from Norway - the Finnmark area in Vardø, to be exact - alleged to have been found at the home of one Kirsti Sørensdatter, who was burned at the stake after the witch trials of Vardø in 1621. She was condemned by her neighbour Mari who claimed that Kirsti was a daughter of the devil. She came to Mari in the night, threw a fox skin over her and transformed her. Then the two of them flew to Satan's Christmas Party.'

'Was it fancy dress?' Kaspar asked.

'I'd leave the jokes to me if I were you,' Sven said.

'This is no joking matter.' The voice came from the doorway where their boss, Kriminalkommissarie Bergen stood, frowning, his white hair gleaming against his tanned skin, the happy result of a policing conference in Barbados. 'Two more bodies have been found – a 54 year old retired police officer Erik Wilsson has been found in Landskrona, hanged from his bedroom window with a sheet and an elderly woman, Else Jørgensdatter, has been found in Vardo with her tongue cut out and tied with a ribbon round the middle. The book of spells was open on her stomach.'

'That might be some kind of a warning,' Sven said. 'The Devil is said to tie the tongues of witches so they couldn't cry or confess unless they faced the ordeal of water.'

'Cause of death?' Anna asked.

'Exsanguination,' Bergen replied, grimly. 'And you should know that both murders pre-dated ours by at least a day, according to their pathology reports.'

'Great. So now we have a serial killer who must have had prior access to the museum...' Anna said. 'And not just in our jurisdiction.'

'The Vardø and Landskrona police are content for us to deal with this,' Bergen said. 'I'm assuming that their resources are as limited as ours. The press are prowling, so we need to get a result on this, fast. Anything so far?'

Anna looked over to Jonsson. 'Enough for a profile?'

He shrugged wearily, - though to be fair, thought Anna, he would have done that if you'd told him he'd won the lottery.

'Methodical, having planned the thefts, so it's unlikely to be a youngster. He would have needed strength for the axe murder though, so not an old person either - someone of a large build suffering from a form of psychosis. The stolen items begin as his trophies but unusually he doesn't take them with him but leaves them at the scene as signatures. He's conveying a message of some kind. I can't be sure what at this stage. I need to visit the scenes really.'

'Not necessary...'Bergen said crisply. 'We have video and crime reports. Time is of the essence and I don't want you to waste yours travelling.' He handed over a couple of DVDs and a sheaf of papers to Anna and left the room. 'Oh by the way the victim's family is here and they want to speak to you, Anna. I hope that's all right...smooth the way and all that.'

Anna nodded. It wasn't ideal but still she could see Bergen's point. They were the ones who had lost the most after all. She turned to the rest of the team and issued them with their instructions 'Sven, follow up on the other two victims...their backgrounds etc. See if we can establish a connection. Jonsson, a more detailed profile please, once you've viewed all the material.

Kaspar, let's review the evidence from all the killings for forensic leads. I want to know for certain if the artefacts match the ones stolen from the museum.'

She left them to it and walked upstairs to what sounded like something impressive - the victims' suite – but was in reality a small room with a few shabby armchairs and a coffee machine in it. She peeked through the door and saw a middle-aged woman sitting there, staring into the distance. She looked careworn, defeated. Her hair was unkempt, her eyes red from crying. She was wearing a pair of jogging pants and a stained hoodie, both of which had seen better days. Standing behind her was a young man in a suit. 'Please God, not a lawyer,' Anna muttered under her breath as she opened the door and walked in.

'Mrs Hartmann?'

The woman began to struggle to her feet. Anna waved a hand awkwardly at her. 'Please, don't get up.'

'What are you doing about this case?' the young man asked. Everything about him was hostile, Anna noticed...from his tone to his posture – leaning forward with his hands clenched – and of course his expression. His eyes shone with a kind of fervour that Anna had only previously experienced in terrorism suspects, during her secondment to the counter-terrorism unit a few years ago.

'We are trying our best to solve it...' Anna said patiently. 'And you are?'

'Nils Hartmann...'

'My son,' said the woman 'and I am Lisbeth Hartmann.'

'I understand you wanted to speak to me?' Anna said.

The woman nodded. 'Why...how did it happen? They wouldn't tell me. We haven't even been allowed to see his body!"

Anna sighed. Relatives always seemed to want to know every detail because they imagined it would help them. And of course sometimes it did; but in a case like this, the details were better left to the pathology report. 'He was attacked...'

'How...with what?' asked Nils Hartmann. The aggression in his voice was palpable.

Anna paused, wondering whether or not to reveal the grisly details.

'We must know...please...' Nils Hartmann said. His hostility was now more like desperation.

'With an axe...'

'In what way?' Nils asked.

Anna looked at Mrs Hartmann, whose eyes focused on her, silently pleading for the truth.

'He was decapitated.'

Mrs Hartmann cried out and then began to sob gently. Her son put a comforting arm on her shoulder. He looked up at Anna. 'Thank you,' he said, all hostility gone. 'We had to know. Do you understand?'

She stared at him, not understanding at all. 'Do you have any other family members to call on?' she asked in the caring voice she used on such occasions.

'Yes,' Nils Hartmann said. 'My uncle Anders.'

'Would you like me to call him for you?'

Nils gave an odd little smile. 'That would be a very good idea.'

Anna got up to leave. As she reached the door she felt a hand on her arm and something was pushed into her hand. 'You should have this. It was in Dad's bag. He took it everywhere with him... said it was his birthright. We never knew what he meant.'

She nodded and left. As she walked down the stairs back to the Squad she looked at what she had been given. It was a small paperback book – 'Nordic Noir: The Real Stories'.

The Odd Squad HQ buzzed like a hive. Sven was peering intently at his computer screen. Kaspar was shuffling papers, evidently looking for something and Jonsson was typing furiously. They scarcely noticed Anna as she sat at her desk and started to flick through the book. Then she, too, went to her computer and started to search.

The door opened and Bergen came in. 'We've found the head.'

'That's good...' Sven said. 'It might give us a lead.'

'That's bad, actually,' Bergen said. 'Anna, you and Sven need to go back to the museum right now.'

Twenty minutes later they were standing by the broken display cabinet that had once contained the axe used to execute Anna Mansdottur.

'Anders Nilsson-Hartmann, come out with your hands up where

we can see them please,' Anna shouted. She and Sven stood with their arms outstretched, each carrying a gun.

A figure emerged from the shadows. It was a large, avuncular looking man with a big welcoming smile on his broad face, a large knife in one hand and the decapitated head of Harry Hartmann in the other.

'Hi, how are you?' he said.

'Hi Anders, I'm fine. How are you?' Anna said.

'What is this, a tea party?' Sven muttered under his breath.

'Anders, you know it's all over don't you?' Anna said carefully.

'No, no it isn't. There are still some more to kill. I have to finish. You must see that...' Anders started to laugh – a chilling empty sound – devoid of any real feeling. 'There is Johan Ander – the murderer and robber - he was guillotined - his grandson lives in Malmo. I've made him his own guillotine - it comes in a flat pack... want to see it?'

Anna inched closer. 'No Anders, it's over. Do you understand?'

'Then there's Lindberg - they executed him even though he didn't kill anyone, but still, his great, great granddaughter might so that needs to be sorted out. So many...so many...'

'No. It stops here,' said a voice from behind them. Nils Hartmann walked forward until he reached his uncle and embraced him. 'You've done enough now. Give the knife to me, Uncle Anders.'

Anders dropped Harry's head and put his hand on his nephew's shoulder. 'I can't Nils. Not yet. There's one left that has to be dealt with and only I can do it...'

Nils stared down in horror as his uncle tightened his grip and lifted the knife.

'You are the last in the line, Nils.'

'Please, Uncle Anders...don't do this. I am not a killer. I would never hurt anyone. You know that...really, don't you?'

Anders hesitated as he considered his nephew's plea. Anna tensed to make sure of her aim but, before she could shoot, Anders pushed Nils away, took the knife and sliced through his own throat. He fell to his knees as the blood gushed from his neck. Then he was gone.

'Explain...' ordered Bergen, sitting back in his chair. Anna did not answer but pulled the book that Nils had given her out from her back pocket and started to thumb through the pages.

'This is a book that was being written by the killer – Anders Nilsson-Hartmann. It's a study of true crime. Listen."

She reached a particular chapter and started to read.

'Hilda Nilsson, the angel maker – child murderess who hanged herself with her own bed sheet in her prison cell.' She flicked through to another page... 'Anna Mansdottur, executed by decapitation for the murder of her daughter in law.'

Sven put his hand up as if he was in a classroom. Anna tended to have that effect on people, she'd noticed.

'I did a bit of reading on the case," he added. 'Apparently there was some doubt about the conviction. Anna may have been framed by her son, Pers Nilsson.'

'There's also Kirsti Sørensdatter,' Anna added. 'As you mentioned Sven, she was burnt at the stake as a witch having been condemned by her neighbour, Mari Jørgensdatter, who said that Kirsti had given her a book of spells.'

'And that's all in this book he was writing?' Bergen asked.

Anna nodded and held it up. Sven squinted at it and began to read out the title. 'Nordic Noir: The Real Stories, a compendium of Scandinavian crime scandals written by...Anders Nilsson-Hartmann.'

Anna looked at them. 'Harry told Anders about his new job and Anders decided that it would be an ideal opportunity to write the book he had always wanted to - about Nordic true crime.'

'So what went wrong?' Bergen asked.

'Anders and Harry found out more than they had bargained for. According to the records I found, they were the grandsons of the murderer Pers Nilsson, who, understandably, changed his name to Hartmann when he was released in 1914.'

'When Anders found this out whilst he was researching the book it had a shock so profound that it sent him into a psychotic state,' Jonsson said.

'Indeed,' Anna said. 'Through Harry, Anders found out about other cases and wrote about them. Once the book was finished, he decided to kill the last descendants of each murderer, finishing with his brother and then himself. His nephew Nils started to suspect that something was wrong. When he found out his father had been murdered, he realised what his uncle was doing and gave me the book – even though he couldn't bring himself to tell me why.'

Almost a fatal decision,' Bergen said. 'Still better late than never, I suppose, and he saved himself in the end.'

Anna picked up the Nordic Noir book and took one last look before putting into an evidence bag. In the front was an inscription written by Anders Hartmann. It said:

'Blood will tell,' which for Anna explained it all.

Family tree

V H Leslie

Tyler's mum was wearing the horrendous bobble hat again. It was so poorly constructed with looping loose stitches and gaping holes that she might as well have wound the yarn around her head like a turban. The worst of it was the enormous green pompom, which toppled back and forward as she crossed the playground. Tyler flinched on seeing her and hoped Kevin and Phil hadn't noticed.

'Nice hat, Mrs. Burrows.'

'Oh, thanks Kevin.' She smiled. 'I made it myself.'

'Really? Wow.'

Tyler thought Kevin's incredulity was a bit overdone and would have elbowed him if he'd been closer, but his mum didn't seem to notice. In fact she patted her hat proudly. Tyler and Phil fell in step behind them as they continued to discuss the creative potential of knitting all the way to the car.

'Nice day at school boys?' she asked when they were seated in the old camper. With its cheap paintjob failing to disguise the rust, it was almost as embarrassing as his mum's hat.

'You know, Mrs Burrows, another day another dollar,' Kevin said, buckling himself in. He'd made a habit of using 'grown-up' expressions around adults, which essentially meant mimicking his old man's clichés. Tyler hoped it wouldn't lead his mother into another rant about capitalism but Kevin could do no wrong today. He'd claimed the front seat as usual, his prize for making small talk. Tyler and Phil, on the other hand, were squashed into the back, sitting amongst boxes of cardboard and paper from the recycling bank, the materials from which Tyler's mum would fashion mini works of art in papier mâché.

'And what about you two?' his mother asked, shouting over the rumble of the engine.

Phil maintained his stare out of the window making it clear he wouldn't be participating in any chitchat. It fell to Tyler.

'It was ok,' he managed, hoping she would leave it there.

'Details, sweetheart?' she pressed, and Tyler knew she wouldn't be appeased until he'd mentioned at least one salient feature of his day.

'Um, well, we've been planning our experiments.'

'And what experiments are those?'

'For the science fair, Mrs Burrows,' Kevin chipped in.

'The science fair?' She adjusted the rear view mirror and Tyler met her eyes in the glass. 'And I presume you were going to tell me about this eventually?'

Tyler hoped the question was rhetorical and shifted to look out of the window.

'What's it about?'

'We're analysing blood cells,' said Kevin.

Tyler's mum screwed up her face, the many ethical objections that came to mind visible on her brow. She was vegan in spirit if not in appetite.

'And,' Kevin continued, 'Tyler's been paired with a girl!' He laughed but it was exaggerated and Tyler suspected it contained a degree of envy. Because it wasn't just any girl he'd been paired with, but Janie Tailor. Blonde and slim and beautiful Janie Tailor. The only girl in school with the unmistakeable budding of breasts, with the exception of tubby Shanice Bolton, whose obese rolls provided cleavage to rival any surgically enhanced celebrity.

But Tyler wasn't feeling lucky. Science was his favourite subject and having a new partner, and a girl at that, was proving a distraction. It didn't help that she had lots of opinions. He'd been used to working with Phil and Kevin, whose apathetic involvement usually allowed him to work entirely on his own. Just as he preferred.

'Ohhhh. What's she like, sweetie?' his mother asked.

It was for this reason that Tyler preferred reticence. He didn't want to face a barrage of questions on a subject he vaguely understood himself. Girls were a mysterious species, communicating with eyes full of giggles and shyness and knowing. And later they'd turn into creatures that in some ways resembled his mother. That was the most perplexing part of all.

It was easier to act the part of a typical adolescent; he shrugged. 'She's alright.'

'My goodness, Tyler, you'd think I'd brought you up without any refinement,' she sighed, pulling into the driveway. 'Are you like this at home, Kevin?'

Kevin cast a superior glance into the back of the camper and smiled.

'Certainly not, Mrs Burrows.'

*

Tyler opened the fridge and grabbed three cartons of pomegranate juice. His mum was setting the table, sweeping sketches, palette knives and paintbrushes onto chairs. She laid the table slowly with an artistic eye. Plates laden with pita bread and falafel, bean salad, hummus and olives were arranged as if they were part of an exhibition. Tyler looked at the spread and rolled his eyes. Why couldn't they have chicken nuggets and spaghetti hoops like other children?

Not that he would dare tell his mum how many chicken nuggets he consumed at Phil's house. He knew she'd call the whole thing off if she found out he was living on a diet of junk food. Whenever Tyler returned from Phil's he'd tell her he'd eaten cottage pie again, something bland and wholesome, too dull to raise suspicions. No doubt Phil did the same, substituting tajine with toad-in-the-hole when quizzed. Phil's mum was as fearful of the spice being stirred into her son's life as Tyler's mum was of the absence of it. He realised that the whole arrangement pivoted on a delicate foundation of wilful deception.

The arrangement was part of the imaginatively named 'Parent Share', an ingenious plan to parcel out their parental responsibility once a week in exchange for one blissful night off. Of course if Tyler's mum could rely on Tyler's dad there wouldn't have been any need for the arrangement. But as it was, Tyler liked going to Kevin and Phil's and getting as close to normalcy as possible.

Tyler's mum liked it too. It was marked on the calendar as 'Marian's Time Out' though Tyler objected to the insinuation that he was something she needed time out from. When Tyler returned home from either Kevin's or Phil's, the house would be littered with trinkets to attain inner calm – candles, crystals, incense. The drawback was that two nights a week her inner-calm was countered by the presence of three raucous boys instead of one.

At least they could play in the garden.

'Tell the boys to stay near the house,' Tyler's mum called as Tyler bounded out of the back door cradling three cartons of juice.

'It's nearly dinner time.'

*

Tyler ran across the lawn to Kevin and Phil. They were kicking a football back and forth. Kevin, slightly overweight for his age and without any aptitude for sport, was putting a great deal more effort in than Phil who returned the ball lazily with his hands in his pockets.

Tyler liked the garden. There were elements that weren't to his taste - a half finished mosaic mural by the shed, a spattering of lanterns along the path and a pergola that sat snugly and slightly off kilter on the lawn - but luckily Tyler's mother flitted from project to project like an insect to nectar and her attempts to beautify and tame the garden were short-lived. The vegetation had precedence now; the shrubbery was overgrown, concealing a wealth of wildlife, the hedgerows were neglected and wild, and thick foliage at the bottom of garden formed a towering, impenetrable wall.

Kevin passed the ball and Tyler returned it. At what height did a lawn stop being a lawn Tyler pondered as the long grass tickled his shins. Tyler wasn't interested in football but it was an enjoyable challenge in the long grass. The ball compressed the grass it rolled over, forming a series of interlacing paths like an exposed mole tunnel.

'Why doesn't your mum cut the grass?' Phil asked when his shot swerved off centre.

Tyler sipped his juice thoughtfully. Cutting grass was a job for dads.

'Why don't you?' Kevin replied as he retrieved the ball.

'Oi butt-nugget, who asked you?' Phil responded. He didn't speak much but when he did he made a point of creating obscene combinations. And he didn't shy away from the hard stuff either. Tyler remembered when he had called Ben Walker the C-word in P.E. The word had swum in Tyler's stomach for days afterwards; its semantic weight indigestible.

'You should cut it since you love Mrs Burrows so much,' Phil continued.

'Whatever,' replied Kevin, though he kicked the ball as hard as he could. The long grass brought it to a sluggish stop just before Phil's feet.

'Why do you always have to suck up to her so much anyway?' Phil asked.

'It's called being polite, you should try it some time.'

Tyler watched their exchange, emphasized by the kicking of the ball. Kevin broke the monotony with an ungainly punt, which bounced in the long grass and approached Phil mid-air. Phil took the opportunity with enthusiasm and volleyed the ball as hard as he could. It flew into the pergola, rebounding off the canvas, which propelled it further down the garden. It cleared the trees and they heard it crash into the wild grass at the bottom.

'Well done,' Kevin said.

Phil smiled. 'Come on,' he called running for the ball.

'It's alright,' Tyler said, 'I've got another one in the shed.'

'Stop being a wimp,' Phil replied, 'you scared of spiders or something?'

Tyler found himself running to catch up with Phil. Kevin trudged on behind. Tyler wasn't really bothered about spiders but now, delving further into the undergrowth, he saw there were a lot of them. Their speckled bodies rocked precariously on webs as three lumbering boys darted through their terrain.

'Listen, Phil. Let's go back,' Tyler panted.

Before he knew it Phil had disappeared into the wall of green. Tyler and Kevin exchanged glances before Kevin, too, vanished. Tyler followed reluctantly behind, wondering how he was going to explain.

As he emerged he saw his friends staring in disbelief. An

enormous tree house stood three metres or so off the ground. An impressive veranda surrounded it with a ladder that ran up to the entrance. Above the door a lopsided sign read, 'Tyler's Place.'

'It's just the old tree house,' Tyler explained.

Kevin and Phil turned to him with raised eyebrows, shocked at the breach of trust.

'Why haven't you shown us it before?'

'It's dangerous,' Tyler continued, 'we're not supposed to play down this end of the garden.'

Phil and Kevin looked at him in bewilderment and burst out laughing.

Tyler picked up the ball, 'Why don't we go back to the house now?'

'Fuck that,' Phil replied.

'Seriously, Mum said dinner was ready.'

'Who made you the boss?' Phil challenged.

'Shh,' Kevin said.

'Me, it's my house, you have to-'

'Shh!' Kevin repeated, 'I think there's something in there.'

Kevin and Phil crouched lower to the ground and Kevin pointed. 'There. See it?'

A blur swept past the window.

'Seriously guys, let's just go,' Tyler pleaded.

The boys were still looking at the window, so when a figure came out of the door it caught them by surprise. The dark creature stood staring at them, breathing heavily, its hands clutching the railings in a posture of defiance. It was covered in dark hair with matted long tresses running down its back and it stood completely naked, its genitalia dangled obscenely from its nest of pubic hair.

The creature roared.

Phil and Kevin screamed and ran as fast as they could.

Tyler watched them go and shook his head at the beast man. He slumped back to the house to tell Mum.

*

'It will all clear up in a day or two,' Tyler's mum said, passing the bean salad.

Tyler dished a measly spoonful onto his plate, knowing he wouldn't be chastised about his lack of vegetables.

'It won't,' Tyler said. 'They're not going to be able to play here anymore, are they?'

'Well, Phil's dad said probably not.' What he'd actually said was a lot less polite; Tyler had heard when she'd held the phone away from her ear. It certainly accounted for Phil's colourful language. 'But you never know, Kevin's mum is very understanding. Her husband is an alco-hol-ic.' She whispered the last word as if it wasn't suitable to be uttered at dinner.

'At least that's normal.'

'Hardly.'

'More than we are.'

'Now Tyler, your father is entitled to express himself in whatever way he sees fit.'

'Couldn't he do it with clothes on?'

Tyler's mum sighed and spooned more beans onto her plate.

'It's two afternoons a week,' Tyler continued, 'couldn't he put clothes on then? It's not a big ask. Even his loincloth would be better.'

'Tyler, you know your father lost his conception of time long ago. His world is governed by the seasons, not our weekly schedules.'

'Well couldn't we signal to him to put some clothes on when we have friends over?'

'I don't think he has clothes anymore.'

It was pointless arguing. His mother supported, no, encouraged his dad's crazy way of life.

'I mean, what your father is doing is actually very brave, going back to nature. People shouldn't be so scared of embracing their bestial natures. I'd do it, if I didn't have the shackles of motherhood to contend with. No offence.'

Tyler seriously doubted that. For all her talk she was too addicted to hot baths and Freeview to live in a state of nature. And he had to wonder if perhaps she preferred dad down at the bottom of the garden.

*

Tyler carried the bucket slowly down the garden path. He could hear the planks of wood shaking as his father jumped up and down in excitement. When Tyler emerged from the thicket his father leapt from the tree house in one mighty motion to land at Tyler's feet, panting. If he'd had a tail it would have been wagging.

Tyler tipped the bucket up and a slab of raw steak fell to the ground. Like an animal, his father tore at it with his teeth, ripped with his fingernails that were sharp points and scooped it up into his mouth. Blood dripped from his chin and Tyler saw that his hands and chest were still stained dark brown from the last time.

Tyler's mum insisted that his father should have at least one good meal a day. Before he'd given up the ability to speak, his father was adamant that he wanted to survive only on what he could catch. But pickings were slim in the suburbs; there were only so many squirrels to eat. Nobody wanted him to starve so they began to subsidise his diet. Tyler's father turned his nose up at their first offerings; conventional meals were thrown back up the garden path. The only thing he'd eat was raw meat. Most of the time his father would grab whatever meaty morsel Tyler brought him and scuttle away with it, burying it somewhere in the garden to allow it to rot and tenderise. He liked it best this way, unless he was really hungry.

Tyler hadn't wanted to take him his breakfast this morning. He was still angry about his display the previous day. Even animals could be trained to behave civilly and Tyler hadn't given up hope of tempting the wildness out of him. But as long as his mother allowed him to spend his days running around naked and nibbling squirrel cadavers he'd continue to take steps further back down the evolutionary scale.

Tyler remembered his father before the tree house. He used to wear a shirt and tie then, carry a briefcase. Tyler had never been inside, though it bore his name above the door. At first he'd been excited about it, even helped his father sketch ideas. But his father had become obsessed by it. He'd work into the night, building the rafters, laying cladding, varnishing it over and over. It became a monster of a project, becoming larger and more elaborate than any tree house Tyler had ever known. And his father approached it with more commitment than he had ever invested into anything before. He became consumed by the details.

Tyler watched him build whilst other facets of his life crumbled away. He began to work shirtless and it wasn't long before his flabby white torso was transformed into lean muscle. But it wasn't just his clothes being stripped away. He lost all interest in his day job, in his family and his responsibilities. And he didn't seem to mind. It meant he could spend more of his time making the tree house perfect.

His father began to use it as a den. Sometimes he wouldn't even come into the house at all and soon these days stretched into weeks. When the single mattress was put in, Tyler knew his dad had permanently moved out. At first it was as if nothing had really changed - he'd always been evasive presence in the house anyway - only now he was down the bottom of the garden. But Tyler and his mother soon forgot to visit him and the garden became overgrown, obscuring the tree house and separating him from their world. Before they knew it, left to his own devices, Tyler's father had degenerated.

Watching him now, Tyler thought he was witnessing a strange kind of devolution. The tree house wasn't an opportunity to live off the land; it was an oversized kennel that facilitated a transformation into something beastly. His father appeared hairier each time he saw him. And he smelt too. A lingering odour travelled with him, carrying a scent of earth, decay and faeces. He communicated only through a series of grunts. Tyler imagined a time in the future when he'd have a full pelt and his teeth would be sharp carnivorous points. Soon he wouldn't recognise anything human at all.

*

Tyler sat in the science lab. He held a test tube in one hand and a pipette in the other. Janie was recording the results in a neatly lined table that had taken longer to draw than the experiment so far. He'd arrived late to class and the only lab coats left were at the very back of the science cupboard. Janie had insisted he spend another five minutes wiping them down of any cobwebs that may have gathered on them. Tyler didn't care that they were behind their classmates. He didn't care that they'd probably fail this assessment. He didn't care about anything. His mind was preoccupied with thoughts of Kevin and Phil running screaming from his naked father. He'd expected to come to school to be greeted with gibes about his father being a flasher, or about him being the son of Tarzan, but both boys were absent. Too traumatised, probably, by the whole experience.

Tyler suspected his father had a mental problem. There was a counsellor at school and he often wondered what she would make of his father's unique living arrangements. He was pretty sure that mental patients needed to be kept in mental institutions, not a tree house at the bottom of the garden. Granddad hadn't gone to a tree house.

Janie looked up from her table. She blew particles of rubber off the page.

'Aren't you going to start?' she asked.

Tyler placed the pipette into the test tube, extracting the chemical and depositing it on the slide that was already prepped with blood. He pushed the slide underneath the lens of the microscope and peered through the eyepiece without really seeing.

*

Tyler waited at the school gates for sight of his mother's beat-up camper. He looked at his wristwatch for the hundredth time. Surely she hadn't forgotten him. It was usually Phil's mum's turn but that was before his father had behaved, well, like an animal. For a moment Tyler had the dreadful thought that she'd finally sold the camper. She'd been threatening it for months, fed up with the guilt of running an automobile and the pollution it caused. He didn't like the van but before 'Parent Share' she'd seriously considered buying a tandem. Perhaps this was the excuse she needed. Tyler sighed. If there was anything worse than a feral father it was a mother and son in matching fluorescent cycling jackets, bicycle helmets and ankle clips.

After forty minutes Tyler decided to walk home. It wasn't far really. Dusk was beginning to settle, triggering the streetlamps, which slowly flickered to light. As he got closer to home, he became aware of an abundance of posters pinned to lampposts and telegraph poles. Images of tabbies and terriers snapped in red-eyed poses dotted the neighbourhood. So many had disappeared in the last year, as if they'd been hunted to extinction. Tyler sighed and looked elsewhere. Though the sun hadn't completely set, Tyler could see the pale outline of the moon. It was full.

He let himself in the front door, kicking off his shoes in the hall, knowing his mother didn't like him to bring the outdoors in.

'Mum?'

There was no answer. She didn't appear to be in, though the camper was in the drive and her handbag in the hall. He checked the rooms one by one, finding evidence of her here and there, a cup of coffee on the sideboard, her sketchbook open on the table. Tyler walked through to the kitchen and saw with surprise that the back door was wide open.

'Mum?' he called into the darkness.

He placed a tentative step outside; the grass was dewy and made his sock damp. He was about to wander into the garden's depths when he saw a pile of clothing on the ground, a bra laying casually on top in all its feminine effrontery.

And then he heard the noises.

It sounded not unlike his father's growling, a long, guttural exhalation of emotion. But as he listened harder, he could hear another sound, a voice not quite so wild, but uninhibited and familiar. The voices merged together, howling wildly into the night. The sounds became more urgent, quickening and Tyler realised with wide-eyed apprehension that he was listening to the bestial coupling of his parents.

He slammed the door in disgust.

*

Tyler heard humming in the kitchen the next morning.

'Morning, sleepy head,' Tyler's mum called as he descended the stairs. He came down two at a time, hoping to speed up the breakfast process and get out of the door as quickly as possible.

'I made waffles.' She smiled.

Tyler didn't want anything borne of this mood. 'I'm not hungry.'

She placed a plate in front of him regardless. 'And how was school yesterday?'

'Fine, especially when you're the only one there gone five.'

'Tyler, we've been over this,' she said, placing her fork down. 'I've apologised.'

Tyler thought back to the previous evening, to the sound of his mother eventually stumbling back to the house and her tentative knocking on his bedroom door. But he had successfully managed to barricade himself in and his monosyllabic responses had kept her at bay.

She resumed eating, 'I was just a little preoccupied last night.'

Tyler grabbed his lunch box; he didn't want to think about how she'd been preoccupied.

'Will you take your father his breakfast before you go? He'll be ravenous.'

'Can't you?'

Tyler's mother looked at herself in her pink flannel dressing gown and shook her head. 'Not like this.'

Tyler sighed. She was behaving like teenager. 'You could leave your clothes by the door again.'

'Tyler!'

'Well I'm not doing it,' he continued. 'If you want to pretend that this is normal, you can take it to him yourself.'

'Tyler, he's your father.'

'But he isn't, is he?' Tyler yelled, 'He's a beast.'

Tyler's mum cupped a hand over her mouth to suppress a sob. She was an emotional time bomb at the moment and Tyler was happy to be the detonator. She sat down heavily at the kitchen table and let the tears fall.

The feeling of victory was fleeting. He didn't want to leave his mum like this.

'Mum, don't cry,' Tyler began, 'I didn't mean it.' He stroked her dressing gown. It reminded him of fur. 'Forget I said anything. I'll take it.'

Tyler placed his lunch box back down and grabbed the handle of the bucket instead. He pushed the door wide and hurried down the garden path. This was what he didn't like about women, how unfairly they used their feminine wiles to get what they wanted.

As usual, Tyler heard his father before he saw him, the sound of wood thumping and creaking as he jumped in excitement like a baboon. Tyler pushed through the wall of foliage and emptied the bucket onto the earth. His father leapt to the ground with cat-like dexterity. He began devouring the meat in voracious mouthfuls. Tyler sat beside him.

Once, before his father had gone completely feral, Tyler had found him at the bottom of the garden, hunched over a spider's web. Tyler watched him pick off the mummified remains of flies and pop the cocooned bodies into his mouth. After he'd picked the web clean, he'd move onto another one, snacking on the web coated corpses. He seemed slightly embarrassed when Tyler had asked what he was doing.

'They're perfectly nutritious Tyler,' he'd said. But his expression was confused as if he knew something was wrong but couldn't help himself. As if he couldn't help any of it.

Now, watching him devour the meat, Tyler cried quietly, using his sleeves to wipe away his tears. The beast man paused and looked up from his food. He sidled closer to Tyler and sniffed his hair and patted his head. Then he placed an enormous hairy arm around Tyler's shoulders and pulled him into his great earthy body.

*

Janie was in her lab coat already when Tyler got to class. She handed Tyler his with a smile, clearly proud of having braved the science cupboard on her own. She'd laid out the equipment as neatly as his mother would have and had set up the microscope.

'I thought we could make up for lost time,' she said.

Tyler nodded and slipped the lab coat over his uniform. He was excited about the project, eager again to embrace the cold logic of science. He fingered a length of his father's coarse hair in his pocket. He'd taken it from him that morning when he had unexpectedly embraced him. If he could distract Janie, he could pop the hair onto the slide and look at it through the microscope. He wondered what he would discover. If the microscope could reveal the dappled intricacies of a blood cell, what would it be able to tell him about his father? He doubted that the magnification of his father's hair follicle would reveal a lot but he liked the idea of placing it under the lens and under the scrutiny of science. With science on his side perhaps he could uncover the mysteries of genetics, unravel the gene sequence and find some crucial missing link. If he could understand his father, maybe he could cure him.

Tyler thought back to the beast man's strange embrace that morning and of his mother's happy mood before he'd disrupted it. The way she engineered it so Tyler would see his father daily. Perhaps it wasn't the promise of breakfast that made the beast man so excited, that had him banging about on the wood planks, but the opportunity to see his son. Despite the putrid odours, the tickle of matted hair and the blood on his skin, his father had embraced him. And Tyler had liked it. It was something they had never done before the tree house.

A spider, large and black as an inkblot, suddenly darted across the back of Janie's lab coat and into her hair. Without hesitation, Tyler dropped the pipette he was holding and seized the creature from Janie's tresses. Janie jumped at the unexpected contact and Tyler held the spider at arm's length by one twiggy leg.

Instinctively, he popped it in his mouth.

And as Tyler felt the squirming body on his tongue, tasted its juices as he chewed; he finally understood what his father had meant. He swallowed the writhing remains to Janie's screams of disgust, but it left an insatiable taste in his mouth, a new hunger and he suddenly realised that his father had built the tree house for him after all.

(First published in Black Static # 27, Feb 2012)

The night watch

Matt Wingett

"Don't let them intimidate you," she says, smiling reassuringly as they enter the new unit at the hospital.

"Intimidate me? Babies? Little babies?" he chuckles, and sweeps his eyes along the lines of cots pressed against the magnolia walls, noting the curved dome of a newborn's head staring at the ceiling, another's tiny pink fingers delicately formed from warmth and softness.

They're in a building on the hospital grounds that contains an experimental research unit – that's what they told him at the temp agency. *But this room doesn't look all that experimental*, he thinks. He has temped in all sorts of places and there is nothing special about this one.

He steps over to the nearest cot, stretching out his hand to a slumbering bundle. "Hello my little one," he coos. The infant's eyes open at the sound and fix upon his face.

Something in the expression immediately halts his hand. He steps to the next cot, then the next. Each child has the same look. *Watchful. Knowing.*

He shoots an anxious look to his employer, an Asian woman in her thirties with neat, bunned hair.

"What do I have to do?"

"Ensure they're fed. Very simple," she smiles.

"Why do they..." he stops half way through the sentence, seeing more eyes appear between bars. "Why do they stare like that?"

"Because they are the once-dead," she says matter-of-factly - raising her hand sharply to silence him as his complexion drains. "No, no, it sounds more dramatic than it is. Each was stillborn. Or, that's how they would have been described before The Process." She raises a flat palm and gestures the room with a triumphant sweep of the arm implying the benediction that is science. "The Process brought them back, you see. We've been working on it for a good few years, now."

He feels an acid burn in his veins and struggles to breathe a moment. "And *this*, these babies - are the result?"

"Yes. They have very particular needs. So we keep them here."

Thirty pairs of eyes fix unblinkingly on him. Children of a few weeks to two years. Little flaxen-haired girls and bonny African boys, redheads, pale-skins, soft browns. All silent.

"Stillborn..." he tries the word, then looks at them with renewed pity. "Poor little... loves."

The sentence dies in the watchful silence. With a flutter of panic, he thinks, *There'll be a whole night of this.*

She shows him where each baby's bottle is kept.

"We haven't weaned them yet. Something to do with The Process. Try it..."

She watches him offer a bottle to a child which takes the teat sullenly and suckles, its angry green eyes boring into him. A pale ginger child - the oldest of them, with skin that nearly glows white, blue veins snaking beneath it. For a moment the child refocuses from him to her, holding her gaze for two silent seconds. Satisfied, she turns to leave.

"You'll be perfect," she says, switching on the lamp at a little table in the middle of the room and killing the main light.

"You shouldn't get any trouble. Don't fall asleep yourself." Before she leaves, she points to a bookcase with rows of books. "Should you need entertainment."

Alone, he lays the blue-veined child in its cot, and tries the next child. It squirms away from the bottle, silently screwing its face. The next is the same, and the next. He goes to the door for help, and finds no handle on the inside. He bangs and shouts for a few minutes. No reply. With growing discomfort, he turns to see, in the half darkness, thirty pairs of eyes are still weighing him.

He shakes his head and notes how heavy his breathing is. He yawns. At the bookcase, he grabs a handful of books and sits in the well of lamplight.

One book takes his eye. *The Baby Manual.* He opens it for a clue as to what he should do about feeding them.

Inside the front cover is a note written in pencil. It says:
"One becomes many."
He leafs through looking for clues as to what it means. There is underlining on *feeding baby,* on *playing with baby,* on *how baby responds to strangers.* There are more cryptic marginal notes in a cramped hand, saying things like:
"An abandoned house is a home," and "change baby."
Another says in big desperate letters:
"STAY AWAKE!!!"
The room feels airless now and there is more glittering in the half-darkness, like cat's eyes on a road, all directed at him.
    What are they watching for?

*

He wakes into a dream. In the half darkness of the night, the red-haired baby is standing in front of him, its green eyes just above the desk.
    "Hello," it says, with an adult voice neither male nor female.
    He smiles. It's like that tv advert of a child speaking little wisdoms to its dad.
    "Hello," he answers, experiencing an hallucinatory sensation of himself, disembodied - floating. "Why are you out of bed?"
    The child grins, a malicious light in its eyes. Through parted lips, the lamplight reveals sharp white teeth. "Haven't you guessed?"
    "What's to guess?" he smiles, bemused, his gaze held by the child's.
    Its grin grows wider, revealing deep red gums glistening wetly. He feels dimly that there is something he should stop, but his body feels so heavy.
    "It's a test," The pale child answers. "I left you clues!"
    "Clues?" he repeats, an alarm sounding in his brain.
    "We like to give you a chance," the child says.
    It climbs on to the desk and jabs the pages of *The Baby Manual* with a short finger then pushes its face close to his.
    "It's in here if you care to work it out."
    I need to wake up, the thought gnaws at him as he considers the child. It is rolling its eyes.

"I shall have to tell you," it finally says. "Let me explain. When you have been seeking a place to stay for years, travelling through darkness, and you find a warm, empty space, vacated, kept habitable and inviting long after the original inhabitant has left, how can you pass by?" It asks.

"Then you arrive, and find a world of soft warm, moist people; surely, you invite your friends to join you?" it adds. "That is The Process and how it works on the stillborn."

Wake yourself up. Come on! - he thinks stridently

"So," the child says, "your friends join you."

"This is what happened?" he asks. "With The Process? When they thought they were saving the lives of babies?"

The child nods.

"Yes, we have strayed into this world before. The legends of Changelings - and demons. But we've never come like this, thanks to your medical advances and experiments. Science is a wonderful thing. When we are all together like this, so many of us in one place, we find that inviting new friends to this world can be controlled. We no longer wait for vacant homes in the stillborn bodies inside mothers' wombs. No. Instead we take possession of bodies, when we find them unprotected. Alone."

Somewhere in his clouded dream, he senses hands, tiny soft hands tearing at his clothing. Thirty mouths attaching to his body. White teeth digging in.

The pain causes the the room to jump into clarity, and at last he is acutely aware of his surroundings – and himself.

He is a spirit, he realises.

A slender silver cord runs from his forehead to his body which was dragged away to a dark corner of the room while the creature before him kept him engaged. He sees his body... covered with children, sucking life from him. He looks in horror at the husk of himself, shrivelled, a shrunken homunculus with a tail, now the size of a baby. And hovering nearby, disembodied, a dark malevolent shape moving closer, quivering it seems, expectant at its new home.

The child before him laughs again.

"We are evicting you," it says. "Your body has a new tenant."

And with a sweep of its hand, the child breaks the silver cord.

*

The next day, the Asian woman with her bunned hair steps in with a new temp.

"Don't let them intimidate you," she says, half smiling.

Thirty one pairs of eyes are watching.

Foamhorses

Nicola Tyrell

You should see the sunrise here. When the light begins to touch the water it's majestic; the darkness of the sea reborn in living colour. It reminds me of her. Her long, dark hair and the way it seemed to wave in the sunlight, reflecting colours I had never imagined. Her smile, changing from one moment to the next with her mood, but always beautiful. You'll forgive me if I choose to remember her this way, if I choose not to remember the mocking smile that last night, the night when she cut me adrift. She told me I was pathetic, hardly a man at all, that she was leaving me. Maybe she was right. I waited for her. I thought if I gave her some time things could be other than they were. They say she was seen in Manchester, but I know better. There was no going back.

So I came here.

I always liked the sea in winter. There is something mysterious, even dangerous about it. Frightening, yes, but also vital. It's in the nature of man to take risks, and the gains can be great. But I'm not explaining myself properly. I needed a change, and I needed to be somewhere the air smells good. City living suits me, though, so Portsmouth, a city right on the coast, was a natural choice, being just about as far away as I could get from things. Finding a place to stay wasn't easy, and cost me almost everything I had. I have certain requirements; I won't share a bathroom, I like to live in quiet buildings, and I have always kept my own hours. I figured that if I found work quickly, I wouldn't have to compromise on that. But when you don't know anyone work is hard to find, or so I found. I'm not sure I'm qualified for much anyway. I used to work in justice, but not any more. I don't know how many jobs I applied for; how many interviews, how many rejections. I remember the rising panic, how to decide between returning there and the simpler option, letting the sea claim me. Dramatic, I know, but I felt it.

One day, stopping at the historic dockyard to ask directions, I saw the smallest of signs in the corner of the gatehouse window. An odd sign, now I think of it, wrinkled, water spotted and faded, but as clear to me as a freshly printed newspaper. "Now hiring: Evening/Night-time Security Staff. Apply within". I knew right away I wanted that job. The dockyard is literally full of ships from almost every period of history. Proof that man can, and has, conquered the sea. I mean, I'm not a great man, but maybe I can conquer something, maybe something small. As directed, I went into the office to speak to the security manager Mr Roth, who offered me the position almost immediately.

Even sitting down he was tall, and as we talked he made notes constantly on a small jotter pad on his desk. I didn't see him again after that day, but I put that down to him working the day shifts. It turned out that I was exactly the kind of man they were looking for, or so he said. Things were falling into place, and I slept like a baby that night.

I can't help but wonder why I'm even telling you my story. I'm not a hero, I didn't change the world. I was never even much of a storyteller before now. I suppose the only thing my story has is proof that things change, and that you move on. People say you have to deal with your problems or be haunted by them, but they're wrong. Settling into a new routine in a new place did wonders for me. I would walk to work, because the route would take me directly along the beach, stony grey surface fighting the water for survival, now disappearing, then suddenly resurfacing, triumphant for a while. On my luckiest days, the wind would whip the water into a frenzy; primal forces battling the beach for supremacy as I walked by, awed and humbled. And I liked the job, too. I worked during the closing hours, after the tourists and the workers had departed. Sometimes I would find myself completely alone, just me and all those ships. I would patrol the grounds with my torch once or twice a night, checking more for rats than people. My main function, though, was to be there 'just in case', so most of my shift I spent in the security hut, sometimes watching the cameras, mostly reading.

So I settled in to my new routine. I like to think that I wasn't lonely. I'd even found a pub for my days off. A quiet-ish, local, older-man sort of pub near to my house. The kind of pub you feel welcome in even if you don't know anyone. I wouldn't say I was happy exactly, but then, who is? Are you happy? Most of the time, the most we can ask for is to be content, and I was, for a while.

One night, walking home from the pub, I caught sight of her. I knew it wasn't actually her, that kind of thing doesn't happen to real people outside of the television. But just for a moment, from behind, I saw that long, dark hair, reflecting the light of a streetlamp. My breath caught in my throat and I stopped right there on the pavement. Yellow light, but reflecting so beautifully. I didn't see her face. A few days later I saw her again, at the crossing ahead of me, just too far away to catch a glimpse of her face. She crossed and I lost sight, left with a memory of hair. Hair I have always loved, even before I met her. All of the women who have caught my eye over the years had it; the source of all my troubles in so many ways. Hair that seems to submerge itself like the beach under the waves, sinking, and then rising in the wind as the strands fight each other to rise to the top. At first, I thought I was imagining her, the way people do when they've lost someone, haunted by a memory, looking for someone they know isn't, cannot, be there. I tried not to fixate, but the memory of her, the memory of her was so strong, so close to me.

I don't know how long went by before I saw her again. Long enough for me to think I had imagined her, that some kind of imprint she had left upon me was resurfacing. The spring was coming and the sea was calming, as much as something so vast and primitive can be calmed. I had spent my day off walking; this had become my way of relaxing, and I liked watching the people as they went about their business, not even noticing me. Anonymity isn't for everyone, but it suits me just fine. I thought of her, then, how she was the first one to notice me, in the pub where she worked. The others seemed to see right through me, but she knew I was there, right from the beginning. And I certainly knew that she was there. She used to joke that I had followed her to that place, hoping to meet such a special lady. I never told her how close to the truth she had been. I didn't imagine that she would have understood, even if I had been honest with her. Arrogant to assume that any other human can see into your heart, understand you as you are.

Having admitted that I was thinking about her, I guess you'll understand why I thought I had created the image of the woman suddenly walking ahead of me. Long, dark hair, and something about the way she walked, sort of swaying, just like her hair in the wind. I squeezed my eyes tight shut, but when I opened them she was still there. She walked, just ahead of me, and I began to wonder. I don't believe in fate, but isn't it possible that if I found her, that things could be different? That I could fix it? She was gone before I could catch a glimpse of her face. I walked the rest of that day, hoping to see her again, but she was gone, swallowed by the city.

The next time, a few days later, I was ready. What I wanted was to see her face, but I didn't want her to know what I was doing. I didn't want to frighten her. My plan was to be sitting quietly on a bench as she walked past me, giving me what I wanted, without attracting any notice. I just needed to see her face, to know that whatever her hair was telling me, it wasn't her. The gap between knowing and accepting can be as wide and as unstable as the ocean, and it's no different with me. Even after everything, I love her. So there I was, sitting on this bench, wishing I had a dog, or anything that explained what I was doing there, just waiting for her. Not her, I know it wasn't her, but waiting to prove that to myself. I wasn't to get my chance that day; she did walk by, I knew she would. But she took an earlier turning than usual back into the streets and away from the beach. I saw her, far ahead, but my eyesight has never been perfect.

I dreamt of her that night. She was walking just in front of me again, her dark, dark hair flowing, reshaping itself around the face I couldn't see. I sped up, of course, but so did she. Each time I began to overtake her the gap grew again, as if she were the beach, and I couldn't conquer her, despite the power in my legs, despite my need. When I woke, later than usual, I realised that I just had to see her face. I wondered if other people who had lost someone saw them again and again. I couldn't stop thinking about it, and if I didn't do something it would drive me insane. Or perhaps I already was. I assumed that if I could just see her face I could forget her, move on. So I began to spend more time than ever on the beach, building up an idea of her movements, at least in relation to her walking. I discovered a pattern: she walked that way most days, at the same time, just after dark. She was probably walking home from work. I created my own pattern. On my days off I would be on the beach, secretly awaiting her arrival.

At work I was still content, walking the grid of the dark dockyard, sometimes exploring the ships, listening for the creaking, ghostlike sounds that old things make if you know how to listen. At night, increasingly I dreamt of her, walking ahead of me, standing outside of my house, but always with her back to me. I didn't even have the imagination to give her a face, so she never faced me. On one especially disturbing night I watched her standing outside, with her back to me, but as I was watching she split, first into two women, then three, then four and finally five. None of them turned, they just stood there, while I tried to fight my rising unease.

Eventually I took my opportunity. The path along the beach and the road adjoining it were both wide, so as she walked by on the other side, I began to follow her. I just wanted to know where she went. If I knew where she went I could come up with a plan. The street-lights were on, so it was easy enough, staying in the gloom between two lamps while using the light to be sure I could still see her. I was close enough to see her take her usual left turning, and then right, walking down a road that ran parallel to, but sheltered from, the seafront. I kept my distance as she stopped. She rooted in her bag for god knows what, but never turned far enough to show me her face. She was moving again, into a garden, and climbing the stairs to the front door. A largish house, flat-roofed and white-painted, as if transplanted directly from the Med into this English seaside setting. She opened the door, giving me just a glance into the hallway beyond. I thought I could smell perfume, some sort of smell I knew, like a trauma too painful to remember. Then the door closed and she was gone. But now I knew where she went, I had a way to see her.

I knew I was obsessed; that if I was not careful, I would be engulfed, swallowed by it, and I would sink without a trace. I found out that she worked in a pub, quite close to the Dockyard as it

happens. I went in for a drink on my way to work one day. She
wasn't there, but I stayed anyway, just sitting at the bar.

It was a nice pub, maybe nicer than my usual. I thought it would
be a better place to watch for her; I was more likely to get a look at
her face, besides which I wouldn't be following her on the street any
more. I promised myself that I wouldn't. Somehow, things seemed to
be falling into place. It isn't healthy for a man to be behaving how I
had been, but now I could get this sorted, get her out of my head and
get the new start I had been looking for.

Tonight the dream was more vivid than ever. She was outside my
house, visible from my bedroom window. It was dark, and she had
her back to me, an outline illuminated by street-light. She turned
slightly, hair so beautiful as it rippled with a life of its own. I don't
know how long I watched her, a second or an age. She was so still.
After a while she lifted her hand, pointing at something. Pointing at
the dockyard. She vanished, and I woke up. I don't know why, but I
find myself getting out of bed and going to the window.

She's still there. I'm not dreaming now, and she is still there. I
don't know how this can be, but I'm going to find out. I begin to
wonder who has been following who, and still I haven't seen her
face.

Seems this could be my chance. I pull on jeans and a shirt and I
go downstairs, knowing she will be gone when I get to the door. But
she isn't, she's still there. As I walk across the lawn, she moves away,
just like in my dream. But this isn't a dream, and she is there. She's
walking down the path to the beach, and I follow her. Somehow I
know that she wants me to follow her, and now I don't know if I'm
doing the right thing. She slips in and out of focus, the darkness
pouring over her, and then receding, then covering, then receding
again. She's going into the dockyard. How can she be opening the
lock on the gate? I lose sight of her, and for a moment I begin to
panic. What if it is her? What if she has come back to me, and what if
she is waiting for me in there? I'm through the gate now. I'm sure I
just caught sight of her hair as she turns the corner ahead of me.
She's walking down to the edge of the harbour. I know this place
better than her though, I go straight on. That way I'll get there

ahead of her, and I'll finally get to see her face.

I'm wrong though, maybe she knows this place better than I thought. She's there, ahead of me, back still turned. Now is the time. I touch her gently on the shoulder. High tide passes over me, and she turns. It is her. My wife, I could never forget her smile. Her hair has grown, it covers her face somewhat, but it's her. Her skin seems to have tightened on her bones, and although she smiles, her lips are drawn back, exposing long teeth, longer than I remember. Her eyes, which used to be brown, are the colour of foamhorses: after they are born at the crest of a wave, before they sink back into death. As she looks at me she smiles even wider. Her smile is almost exactly the same shape as the gaping slit I made in her neck, matching nicely what I did to her chest. The knife is still there, buried up to the handle in her flesh, and she is still smiling, but now she isn't alone.

The others have come and I know them all; four more of them, long dark hair like a chronicle of my life. I ask them what they want, and as they answer it is the sound of the sea. I can hear the water moving in their lungs and their throats. My wife speaks, a sound like the most primal urge of the water, a sound like terror. A terrible sound that tells me that they want me to suffer, that they are five and I am one. As I took their voices, so they shall give mine to the sea. Like the winter sea, angry and powerful, she tells me that my body will never be found, and that they will be sure I suffer until the end of time, that I will go with them now, to the place where I left them. She draws the knife from her chest so that she can give it back to me, and I know I will go with them. They wash over me, wrapping me in their arms. I feel a sharp pain, and I am engulfed. I am falling into the sea with them, and they have conquered me.

Sometimes the sky's too bright

Maggie Sawkins

The police came the other day. I knew they were coming. That's one good thing about living up here. You can see what's going on. They wanted to know why I hadn't been to school. I heard my mum say, 'He's sick, been sick for days.' That threw them. The tall one, the one with the bulgy eyes like Freddy Kruger, didn't believe her. I could tell by the way he looked. 'Where's he now?' he said. 'At the doctors,' she said, 'went about an hour ago.'

She can be all right sometimes, my mum. But mostly she's a miserable cow. Dossing round the flat all day in her dressing-gown. About the only time she gets dressed is when she goes out for a bottle. I can't get it for her because I'm not old enough. I tried once and the sad git in Alldays threatened to get the police. Skeggsy was hanging about outside so we got some fags, and six boxes of Swan. Skeggsy looks older than me – he gets away with it. I told her I got happy-slapped on the way home. She didn't believe me. But I don't care.

Skeggsy's just texted to say the police turned up at Milton Cross. There's been another incident. Only this time it's the flats in Paradise Street. The whole place had to be emptied. They wanted to know where everyone was on Monday morning. I told Skeggsy I was at the arcade trying out my system. He thinks I'm gonna tell him how I do it. That's why he's creeping.

I've got something to show him when he comes round next. I caught it last Saturday outside the Co-op. It's there in the matchbox. Wrapped up in cling-film. They reckon they can survive anything, even nuclear attacks. I've given it a week.

Everything looks smaller from up here - it's like living in Toytown. It doesn't matter being nearer the sky - when you look up

all you see is black. They reckon you can't see the stars in the city
because of all the street lamps and the rest of the crap. We went to
St. Ives once, when I was a kid. They had millions of stars there.
Stars so bright they burnt pissholes in the sky. My dad bought me a
hotdog from the van and we got a blanket out the car and sat on the
hill. I saw two shooting stars. It was like watching fireworks. On the
way back to the caravan I asked him if I could have a telescope for
Christmas. He said he'd think about it. That's what they always say.

My mum's had a 'phone call. It was some bloke. 'Can I speak to
Dawn, please?' - he sounded a right sicko. She was on there for ages.
I went in to see what was going on but she told me to clear off. Then
she started whispering. Don't know why she bothers. Her last one
was a right screwhead. Mick Maloney. Mick the Moron, more like.
Spent all the time in the gym, trying to build up his muscle. Except
when he wasn't here, strutting around. She thought I couldn't hear
them. But I could. I could hear everything. She couldn't understand
why I didn't like him - what you need's a bloke about the place,
that'll sort you out - then he lost it. She had to wear sunglasses for
two weeks, even when it was raining. She didn't go out much after
that.

I've found out his name - it's Bernie. He's 'phoned up three times
today. I pretended she'd gone to the shops. When she woke up she
asked me if anyone had rung. She looked dead miserable. I felt a bit
sorry for her. Then she started drinking again.

It's been nearly a week now. It's had no food, and no air. And it's
still alive. I unwrapped a bit of the cling film last night and poked it
with a pin from the corkboard. I thought it was gonna jump right
out of the box, but I shut it quick. I've decided to call it Bernie. Also
I've decided I'm not going back to school. Only got five months left,
so what's the point? Shakespeare and poets, that's all they teach
you. They don't even speak English. The only good bit was in the
film, when Macbeth got his head chopped off, and one of them
witches did a moonie. Anyway I've got my system. I made fifty quid
in three hours the other day down the pier. Next year I'm going to
Brighton. There's loads of machines there. Then I'll get away from
this dump.

I don't know what's up with her. She's acting mega strange. She
got up early this morning. Got out the dusters and the polish. Went

mad, cleaning everything, even the pot plant on top of the telly. Then she tried to get in my room, except she couldn't get past the door - I wouldn't let her. She said, 'You could at least open the curtains and empty the bin.' Then she gave me a bag of old bottles. Told me to dump them down the chute.

Just after I got there I noticed the warden hanging around. He wanted to know what I was doing with the matches. 'Having a fag, what d'you think?' I told him. He's a right smeg. The way he looked at me - as if I was crawling. 'We've had enough trouble round here with the likes of you,' he said, 'now sod off.' I dumped the bag of bottles at his feet and went back to the flat. Next time, I thought. Next time.

I read once that one day the sun's gonna explode. Then there won't be nothing left. No flats, no school, no insects, no screwheads, no nothin'. All that'll be left is sky.

She's finished cleaning at last. The whole place stinks of polish and disinfectant. Now she's having a bath. I can't even get in there for a piss. She's definitely up to something.

I can't believe it. I went in to watch the telly while I was waiting for Skeggsy and she's sitting there all dressed up. Black skirt and tights and the leather jacket she got off the catalogue. The one she paid eighty five quid for and never wore. And she had lipstick on. 'What you gawping at?' she said. 'I'm going out - it's about time I went out.' I thought she was gonna cry. She put her hand in her purse and pulled out a fiver. 'Here, love, get yourself a MacDonald's.' I sat there watching, couldn't take my eyes off. Then the buzzer went and she jumped up. 'It's for me,' I said, 'I'll get it.' I beat her to the door. But when I answered, it was his voice. Bernie's.

After she'd gone I went out on the balcony and looked down. They were walking towards a car. It was black with a sunroof. He looked quite old, about fifty, grey hair. He opened the door for her and she got in.

She's hid the 'photo. The one she keeps by her bed. The one they had done in the club, the one where my dad's got his arm round her. When we got back off holiday my dad started acting strange, dressing up, going out. Then one day he said he'd been robbed and they had a row. After he'd gone, the electric went and there was no money for the key meter. We had a house then, with a real fire.

When he came back it was dark. My mum and me were on the settee watching the flames. Then he came over, tried to kiss her. She pushed him off and they started shouting. My school photo fell in the grate. There was a big crack right across my face. My mum said he hadn't been robbed - he'd spent it all on the old scrubber. Then she took her ring off. Threw it in the flames. In the morning I came down and poked around a bit. That's when I found it - covered in ash. It hadn't melted at all. I picked it out and took it up to her. I thought she'd be pleased. But she told me to get lost and started crying again. My dad didn't come back after that.

I went into my bedroom and opened the window. There wasn't a single star in sight. No sign of Skeggsy either. That's when I looked up at the calendar on my corkboard. At nine o'clock it would be one week, exactly. I got the matchbox out of the drawer and opened it up.

It was lying there, dead still, all wrapped up in the cling film. I got the pin and poked it. It didn't move. So I poked it again. A bit harder this time, and it shot right up the end of the box. I shut it again quick. The bin under the window was empty. I thought the nosey cow must have got in and emptied it. I tore some pages out of my maths book and put them in the bottom. I put the box on top. I got the Swans from under my bed. 'Let's see how you get out of this one, Bernie baby,' I said. Then I lit a corner of the paper. It was just beginning to catch when the buzzer went. I leapt up and looked at my watch. If it was Skeggsy, he was fifty-five minutes late. Fifty-five minutes too late. I waited for the buzzer to stop and went to look over the balcony. But it wasn't Skeggsy after all. It was the old bill, the one with the bulgy eyes like Freddy Kruger. He was walking towards his car.

When I got back to my room the paper had gone out. I picked the matchbox from the bottom of the bin and shook it. They reckon they're the masters of escape, that's how they survive. But it was still in there. I could hear it rattling. I put it back quick. I looked under my bed and found some old magazines, ripped the pages up, more this time, and placed them in layers on top of the box. Then I got the matches and lit them, one by one.

I could hear some kids messing around down by the garages, so I shut the window and lay on my bed. The flames were beginning to lick the top of the bin. I started thinking about St Ives again. I closed my eyes and it was just like I was back there on the beach, with the sky and the sea almost the same colour, and the seagulls screeching in my ears. I'm helping my dad build a sand castle, running up and down, collecting water in my bucket. It's so hot I can feel the heat on my face, and there's my mum sitting on the blanket next to us, in her black leather jacket. Then she gets up and starts dancing, right there on the sand, and everyone's looking. And the sun's above us just like a balloon, a bright orange balloon, and it's growing bigger and bigger. I want to catch hold of it and I try to run. But I can't.

Contributors

Maggie Sawkins is the 2013 winner of the Ted Hughes Award for New Work in Poetry. She lives in Portsmouth where she organises Tongues&Grooves Poetry and Music Club and runs writing workshops in community and healthcare settings.

S J Butler's short fiction has appeared in The Warwick Review, Salt's Best British Short Stories, Litro, Paraxis and Untitled. She has written and performed in a community play, overcome her fear of poetry for the Foundling Museum, and read and written for live audiences in tents, pubs and light vessels. She lives in East Sussex.

Dr Glenda Cooper is a writer, lecturer and journalist. Originally from the Wirral, she now lives in south London with her husband and two daughters. She won the 2014 Poetic Republic and Writers' Bureau short story prizes & the 2015 Chalk the Sun Story Slam. She was also a member of the 2015 Theatre 503 community playwrights scheme. The idea for *Kissing Him Goodbye* came from an article she read on William Hawes and the founding of the Royal Humane Society in 1774. Find her at @glendacooper

V H Leslie is a writer, printmaker and PhD student. Her stories have appeared in a variety of magazines, journals and anthologies and her collection of short stories Skein and Bone was published last year by Undertow Books. She is also a Hawthornden Fellow and has recently returned from the Saari Residence in Finland where she was researching Nordic folklore. Her debut novel, Bodies of Water was released by Salt Publishing earlier this year. More information can be found at her website: www.vhleslie.wordpress.com

Ruth Nelson is a stay-at-home parent and spends her days roaming the parks and libraries of Sydney, Australia. She is also a psychologist and social activist. She produces a podcast, the Creating Space Project, using women's stories to explore values. She is previously published in an anthology of essays by female humanitarian workers, Chasing Misery, under the name Ruth

Tessa Ditner 100 word bio: Tessa Ditner writes fiction and nonfiction, mostly comedy and satire. Her published short pieces range from male corsetry to latex couture and coral conservation. Editor of the Portsmouth Fairy Tales book and promenade, Tessa works as Portsmouth's literature worker, looking after the city's writers' hub. Check out tessaditner.com for the latest tales, travels, teaching and lost and found writing tips.

Matt Wingett has written tv plays, stage plays, short stories, articles for national newspapers, poetry, song and novels. He has a strong interest in history, both internationally and in his home town of Portsmouth. He recently wrote *Conan Doyle and the Mysterious World of Light,* an account of the Spiritualist beliefs of Arthur Conan Doyle and continues to publish works by the many talented writers around the Portsmouth area. He also gives public talks on aspects of writing and local history.

A J Noon is a short story writer and occasional poetaster. After a period of exile in the North he has now firmly returned to his birthplace and can be found skulking around historic sites. He has performed at various events in Lancashire and at the Day of the Dead 3 in Portsmouth.

Tom Pinnock spent most of his life getting into trouble for saying the wrong thing. After taking this talent around the country doing stand up, he discovered he didn't actually like travelling.
He took part in the prestigious two year course 'Nuffield Theatre Writers Group' in Southampton, mentored by director John Burgess (National Theatre) and regularly appeared on stage at his local Amateur Dramatics Society. He enrolled in the UK's first comedy degree at Southampton Solent University, and after much work in TV, Radio, Animation and Stage Play creation, was awarded his (BA

Hons) in 'Comedy: Writing & Performance'. Tom lives in Hampshire with his lovely wife and ten-year-old monster.

James Bicheno writes historical and alternative historical fiction while dabbling in short stories of different genres (like this one). When not writing he is teaching himself how to draw, cook and run without injuring himself. He is currently working on a series of alternative historical novels set in the seventeenth century and can be found on Twitter somewhere as Jim_Bish.

Christine Lawrence self published her novel *Caught in the Web* at Completelynovel.com and on Amazon as a Kindle ebook. She was one of the authors involved in the Portsmouth Bookfest 20x12, and has short stories published in *Portsmouth Fairy Tales for Grown Ups*. She has performed her writings at many events including Day of the Dead I, II & III at The Square Tower, The St. Valentines Day Massacre, and the Victorious Festival. She writes regularly for Portsmouth's The Star and Crescent at www.starandcrescent.org.uk and is presently working on her second novel *Payback*.

Jacqui Pack's fiction has appeared in a variety of publications, including Litro Online, Swarm, Storgy, and Synaesthesia. She was among the winners of The London Magazine's 2013 'Southern Universities Short Story Competition', was awarded Long Story Short's 'Story of the Year 2009', and holds an MA in Creative Writing (Distinction).

William Sutton is a novelist, musician and Latin teacher. He has performed at the Edinburgh Festival and in Highdown Prison, played cricket for Brazil, and hosted the Day of the Dead performances at Portsmouth Square Tower. He plays accordion with chansonnier Philip Jeays and cricket for The Authors CC. His second historical mystery Lawless and the Flowers of Sin was published by Titan Books in July 2016.

Sue Shipp is a writer. She holds an MA in Creative Writing (Distinction) from the University of Portsmouth. In 2014 she was among the winners of The London Magazine's "Southern

Universities Short Story Competition." Her fiction has been featured in Flash: The International Short-Story Magazine, FlashFlood, and 'The Elizabethan Noyses' of Wymering Manor' part of the Much-Ado-About-Portsmouth Festival in 2016. She is currently involved in a writing collaboration for Voices at the Kings Theatre, and the completion of an historical novel.

Jennie Rawling is an actor and writer from Yorkshire, currently living in London. She writes short stories and articles while trying to focus on writing her first novel, trained for an acting career at East 15 Acting School, and has worked in Spain, Italy and Russia. She is also currently studying for the NCTJ Diploma in Journalism, and blogs about her creative projects at www.scribblesandshakespeare.wordpress.com.

Margaret Jennings is a writer and poet who has had success with competitive story telling and poetry reading. She reads regularly at public events and has performed at festivals. She was long-listed for the Bare Fiction Literary short story prize 2014, and two of her stories have been performed by the White Rabbit Theatre Company. Margaret earned an MA in creative writing at the University of Chichester in 2001 and is currently working on her second novel *Ten Tricks.*

Diana Bretherick is no stranger to crime. She was a criminal barrister for ten years before counselling offenders in the prison system and lecturing in criminology and criminal justice at the University of Portsmouth. She is now a full time writer with crime in both fact and fiction as her subject. Her first novel 'City of Devils' won the Good Housekeeping first novel competition in 2012 and was published by Orion in 2013. Her second, 'The Devil's Daughters' came out in paperback in 2016. She lives in Southsea with her husband and two small but very destructive cats.

Alan Morris a retired postie, is often described as short and ghastly, writes mainly flash fiction. He has been previously published by brilliantflashfiction.com. Alan loves the roar of grease paint and the smell of the crowd at various open mike nights. One day he is determined to finish his fairy tale novel, but not today, in the meantime he is busy scribbling horror sci-fi crime and often a mixture of all three.

Justin MacCormack was born in Glasgow and currently lives in Portsmouth, where he studied film at university. You can always make him squirm with embarrassment by reciting one of his early short stories, of which he has been writing since childhood. His hobbies include painting little bits of plastic shaped like knights, playing board games, running the Portsmouth Guild of Role-players (blatant plug), and complaining that kids these days don't know what's what. Aside from a bunch of embarrassing erotica novels written under a pseudonym that he refuses to disclose, Justin's work has been published by Ionic Books, including his coming of age comedy "Diary of a gay teenage zombie".

Nicol Tyrell is a writer, musician and horror film fanatic from Southsea. She has a degree in English Language and Literature and is currently undertaking research into apocalypse fictions and traumatic dislocations to national identities. Nicola is loathe to discuss herself in the third person, but can be persuaded to do so from time to time.

Lightning Source UK Ltd.
Milton Keynes UK
UKOW05f2218201016

285775UK00001B/49/P